R.I.C.O VOL. 1

COREY BRYANT

Bryant publishing

Copyright

Introduction

Introduction to R.I.C.O.. Enter the world of ex-convicts, Mexican cartel, drugs, sex, entertainment, violence, and death. Meet Antonio Deangelo, an ex-convict turned record label owner/entrepreneur / kingpin. Leader of a ruthless organization called RICO in which stands for Real Individuals' Caliber On high. Come walk down the glamorous but bloody path of Big Business! Legal Business as well as Illegal Business! The Author which would be me, Corey Bryant created this story while incarcerated in the Alabama DOC (Department of Corrections) for 27yrs straight from pure imagination and as a form of escape. As well as exercising my gift from God in which I discovered I had in the Belly of the Beast!

Part I

"Back to Liiife, Back to Reality!"
-By Soul II Soul

Prologue

Damn!! I guess you can say this shit is ironic. Ironically stupid, or maybe even janky as fuck! That is to name this organization after one of the most feared law statutes the U.S. government can come up with. To lock people up for a loong time! But nevertheless, it is what it is... R.I.C.O! Real – Individuals – Caliber – On – High! That means a click of Real-niggaz, but high caliber, Real niggaz!! Big money getting niggaz! The majority of us, are Real-Street-Niggaz. Street Niggaz who love to get money, but got sense enough to get educated. To become entrepreneurs one way or the other with the same abbreviation as the government's united states code annotated title 18.1961-Chapter 96-Racketeer Influenced and Corrupt organizations.

The federal judge reads the indictment and definition off as follows... "Oh yeah... You hear it Right, Indictment!" Racketeering activity* means (A) Any act or threat involving murder, kidnapping, gambling, arson, robbery, bribery, extortion, dealing in obscene matter or dealing in controlled substances or listed chemicals which is chargeable under state law and punishable by imprisonment for more than 1 year. (B) Any act which is indictable under any of the following provisions of Title 18 U.S.C Section 201 (Relating Bribery) Section 224

(Relating to Sports Bribery) Section 471, 472, and 473 (Relating to Counterfeiting) and "Damn!!" I know I don't fit in all this shit this is cracker Reading Off."

Is what I said to myself... and he continues..."Pattern of Racketeering Activity – requires at least 2 acts of Racketeering Activity one of which occurred after the effective date of ... This is got to be a bad dream." I mumbled to myself and he continues "After the commission of a prior act of racketeering activity. "Enterprise" includes any individual partnership corporation, association, or other legal entity." "Do you understand this indictment, in which I'm reading to you Mr. Deangelo?" said the Federal Judge Barret Thomas , of the Northern District of Georgia.

"Yes sir." I humbly answer When all the time, I wanted to say: "Fuck nawl, I don't understand!" And he continues, "The next indictment Mr. Deangelo is under 18 U.S.C.A. 2-848 often referred to as the King Pin Statute. CCE, Continuing a criminal enterprise. You are charged with 1 count of that. Now, I am going back to the RICO charges and read the counts in which you are charged and indicted for."

"I can't believe this shit!" Is what I'm saying to myself.

"You and your organization are charged with 105 counts of racketeering activity. As I explained to you earlier Mr. Deangelo what constitutes racketeering activity and what is a pattern of racketeering activity. Ten counts of murder are linked to you and your RICO organization, in which took place on..." The judge is reading off these charges and indictments of murder and everything else they can pin on me and my click. Seventeen counts of gambling in the form of running an illegal gambling operation from and through sports bars and gambling houses. With illegal bookies taking in money for what they call "Slick Picks", which coincides with the bribery... sports bribery, in the form of point shaving, in college and professional sports. A couple of the athletes who is there to testify for the government shift uneasily in their seats, as all eyes turn or cut their way. Shouldn't have fucked with them Square Bitch Ass Niggaz! Although, it was some real niggaz-stand up guys who were athletes who didn't flip on me. So, I got to be kind of thankful.

"Twenty counts of sports bribery in college sports and professional sports mostly in the form of point shaving. Twenty counts of extortion." My lil young partner Brainhead is sitting there with a smirk on his face like "Fuck it!" While crossing his arms a little above his forehead in what they call the maxed-out sign. He wasn't bullshittin, he and his goons with their T.S.I. Thing. "Turn Something In" extorting niggaz out of their work and money! Yea I was living like Young Jeezy say "My goons got goons!" Tried to cool them young niggaz down, and get them on the tip of drama only when necessary.

"Five counts of kidnapping" read the federal judge. In which was linked to a branch of this RICO organization called "T.S.I", and I'm thinking to myself "All these niggaz who was so-called extorted or kidnapped or both, was supposed to be some gangstaz, and now they got a nigga in court, about to testify on them!

"Ten counts of bribery, ten counts of dealing in a controlled substance". All of these counts and charges are in direct correlation to your "Legal" enterprise entity corporation, Deangelo Enterprises to the furtherance of the conspiracy of your criminal enterprise Mr. Deangelo." Said the Federal

Judge, pausing and taking off his glasses for effect. "In a six-year period. You understand what's going on Mr. Deangelo?" asked the Judge.

"No... not to this point," I answered, wondering why do they ask all these dumb ass questions. I guess it's for the record.

"Well... I hope you will after this trial with the help of your legal team, Mr. Deangelo, because you're in a lot of trouble!" said the Judge.

I got lawyers on Deck! Some of the Best in the Country, so I'm not Tripping. But let me take you back a few years, to paint this picture, to show you how this R.I.C.O thang started. The rise and fall, of one of the most powerful, organized Dope Clicks in America. In the Southern part of the U.S. of A, since BMF!!

Chapter 1

(6 YRS. EARLIER)

As I entered the courtroom, I can feel the eyes of the spectators drilling holes through the side of my face! As if they're trying to read my mind or otherwise read the expression on my face. And I'm thinking to myself, damn, how in the fuck do all these people know that I got a reversal on my case and a new trial? Maybe all these years in prison, got me paranoid! Nawl-cause I recognize a few faces, like my high school sweetheart... Ms. Stephanie Garrison. My ex-girlfriend might know through that Facebook bullshit. Damn! I did post some shit about me, soon to be released from this shit! But how did they know the exact court date?

Anyway, Stephanie went south on me in crunch time. At the beginning of this whole ordeal. I guess she didn't think that I would ever get out of prison! Ha!! And she had married a Detective... Narcotic Detective! Anyway, I had caught a murder case, got out on bond, and got indicted with some of my partners out of my hood, along with some of our partners from Alabama and New York for conspiracy to traffic cocaine with the intent to distribute.

Now, all this shit happened back-to-back, fucking around in these small towns in Alabama. Hustling with some of my cousins from there putting them on, niggaz got jealous, thinking we trying to take over. Because we fucking their girlfriends and getting paid. They brought the drama and one of their heroes ended up getting his face and chest split in half! Closed casket! Now the detectives, knowing that all of this drama is drug-related and coming from some out-of-town niggaz got the feds involved.

Matter of fact, the feds were already involved, because they were already hot on one of my partners' cousins from New York, Dwight. The shit rolled downhill! Long story short, I ended up with fifteen years in the fed and forty years for murder in the state of Alabama. At first, they had my sentences running wild. That means consecutive.

Then, my lawyer got them ran together. Still, my sentence for murder was from a fucked up guilty plea! I plead guilty to a sentence of fifteen years, but when I went to court in the following two months, I was over-sentenced! I fought that issue for years pro-se. That means without a lawyer.

Me being me, I stayed scheming and hustling until I schemed up on me a lawyer, who would help me. My ex-attorney's ex-wife! Ain't that something? They had been divorced. He, my ex-lawyer ended up getting disbarred, and publicly reprimanded, for some shady dealings dealing with some Auburn University students. Yeah, I played on her sympathy in which she showed towards me and my situation when I contacted her. She also showed me something else... She was thirsty and lonely for a man. A Black man at that! So, I put the mack all the way down, got her to file some post-conviction petitions for me, and here I am, back in court.

About to give these devils this time back, just like they gave it to me. By the way, the feds already had me in their custody. I did my time there and was transferred to the state, to a state facility to do my time until I made parole or whatever. But I never made it because I'm back in court.

"Hi Antonio! How are you doing?" Smiled my attorney, Janice Riddlesburg, as we shake hands and take our seats in the conference room of the Jefferson County Circuit Court Room in Birmingham, Alabama where I caught the murder case.

"Hey Janice!! I'm doing just fine." I answered.

"Congratulations!" said Janice. "The Criminal Court of Appeals finally granted you a reversal on your sentence. So, what's about to happen is Judge Pinson is going to bring you a deal for a sentence of fifteen years, and if you take it, he'll sentence you to time served."

"That's a beautiful thang!" I said to Janice smiling like a Chess Cat. "Is they gone let me go today?" I asked.

"Yes!" Said Janice, "All you have to do is go through the formalities for the record, and he'll release you."

"That's what's up!" I answered. As I casually leaned back in my chair rubbing my hands together like Baby, the CEO of Cash Money Records. My family was there! My mother, sisters, daughter, nieces, and nephews.

"Uncle Antonio!" Hollered my badass niece, Ni-Ni. I looked back and smiled at my fam, winking my eye.

It's been a long time coming!

"All rise." Said the bailiff as Judge Pinson comes from his chambers to his seat.

"You may be seated." said the Judge. "This is case #90-744, in the style of post-conviction proceedings. Mr. Deangelo to the Criminal Court of Appeals finds that your sentence was illegal, due to an induced guilty plea and remanded it back to this court for a new trial." "Now from my understanding, I see where a guilty plea has been prepared in place of a new trial. A guilty plea for fifteen years for murder." "With time served." Slowly said the Judge. "Is that what you want to do Mr. Deangelo?"

"Yes, your honor."

"For the record," said Judge Pinson on this 20th day of January, I sentence Mr. Antonio Deangelo to a fifteen-year sentence for murder. So, with the fourteen years, eleven months, fifteen days Mr. Deangelo served in the federal penitentiary. Along with the fifteen days he served in Pre-Trial Detention, before making bond on this case equals up to fifteen years. I hereby release you from incarceration.

"Baaack too Liife, Back to Reality!" An old-school classic from Soul-2-Soul is the first thing that plays in my mind!

"Court adjourned. You are free to go Mr. Deangelo."

I stand up, feeling like a gorilla has been lifted off my shoulders. "Thanks Janice! Thanks a lot!" I tell my lawyer, as I hug her.

"Your welcome Antonio," said Janice, but before she releases her embrace she whispers in my ear. "Tonight, at my place, after you spend time with your family. You have my cell phone number."

I just smiled and backed away from her. "I got ya Janice," is what I told her and walked over to my family and welcomed their hugs and kisses.

My whole bid, all I was focused on was getting out and getting to the money C.R.E.A.M money, and the power, on a big level, and how I was going to implement my plan to get it. Now, it's on!

Chapter 2

(3-MONTHS LATER)

BOOM, BOOM, BOOM! Echoes this .44 Bulldog, As I unload it into the Mexican-Snitch's son! Already getting bout my paper! "Cover him up Chee-Chee." That is what I tell my partner as soon as the victim fell in the six-foot hole which was specifically dug for him.

I was performing this hit for my Mexican partner, I met in the Federal U.S.P. United States Penitentiary out in the Terre-Haute, Indiana and out in Ft. Leavenworth. In fact, up in Terre-Haute, is where our bond was solidified. Garcia Abregado was doing a life sentence for an 848-CCE Conducting A Continuing Criminal Enterprise – The Kingpin statute! Garcia was a bad muthafucka when it came to getting that money when he was free. Cartel Boss! He had done got indicted out of Houston, Texas in the mid-'90s along with a lot of more co-defendants. One of these co-defendant's son is the poor victim who is laying in a hot grave being covered with dirt in a Mexican Desert. Carlos Desendez was high up in rank in Garcia's organization.

When the Feds were looking for Garcia causing him to go underground. Carlos Desendez acted as the intermediary middleman through which other members of the group in-

13

cluding two of his main Lieutenants went to meet with Garcia. It's a shame because Carlos Desendez informed the Mexican authorities where Garcia was hiding! His main man! Covetousness, fear, greed, and sheistyness, made him flip. Besides him being scared to face the consequences, he also was a snake! Wanting Garcia's position and life, he had no problem being the government's star witness.

He got a Rule 5K1.-A Rule 5K.1 is a motion filed by the prosecution to reduce the sentence of a witness based on the witness's cooperation and substantial assistance to the government in the arrest or prosecution of another individual. A Rat! This shit had Garcia hot as a firecracker, I later learned once our friendship had just begun, when we used to be in the law library. All the time, at the same time, researching our case out at Leavenworth over discussing some law issues Garcia started opening up about his life.

About how he got started hustling weed in the late '70s and how he moved into the cocaine game, in the '80s. A real cocaine cowboy, and how he ultimately met his demise. He slowly but surely started revealing how much dope he was moving. I found out that this little Mexican was responsible for tons of cocaine in the United States.

I was astounded. He started trusting me enough to read some of his paperwork and showing me pictures of ranches, mansions, and foreign cars. Amigo was on!! Where our friendship most definitely tightened up was at Terre Haute.

I had left Leavenworth before him and nine months later he was there. Anyway, both of us liked to work out, but we worked out by ourselves. This particular day Garcia was by himself doing his normal routine and I was doing mine. I was on the Dip Bar and he was at the Pull-Bars. I noticed some big ass white boys, about four of them, approach Garcia at the Pull Up Bars. These white boys were A.B. Aryan Brotherhood, which was kind of deep up in Indiana. They hate blacks and Mexicans especially, and whoever else ain't white.

"Anybody on this with you amigo?" Said one of the big white boys speaking on the Pull Up Rack.

"No." Answered Garcia.

"Let us get in with you." Said the white boy. Garcia nodded his head and kind of stepped back. The white boys were doing their sets but, was goofing off at the same time, playing and shit.

"Excuse me." Said Garcia, as he was trying to get to the Pull Up Bars.

"Well excuse me, amigo! I was going to get out of your way!" "Don't get your panties all in a wad over nothing!"

"What?!" Said Garcia. "Look you all can have the Pull Up Bars I'll go somewhere else."

"No... come on back wetback!" Said one of the white boys.

Garcia didn't like that insult. He stopped dead in his tracks and turned around. "Fuck you!" "I'm a wetback and you're a cracka!"

"What the fuck you say?!" Said the big white boy, as he quickly started towards Garcia with his flunkies in tow. Garcia knew he was outnumbered and outsized! But Garcia was tough! Small, but got plenty of heart. So, Garcia didn't budge! He held his ground when the white boys approached. I immediately got off the Dip Rack and walked towards the drama. When the big white boy made it to Garcia, he pushed him and followed up with a punch.

That's all it took for me! I was on the yard, strapped up with a big ass prison knife, so I took off on the big white boy A.S.A.P.! By the time he had done punched Garcia, damn near knocking him down, and grabbed Garcia by the collars about to sling him, I was gagging the big white boy and slapping him in his face with the knife at the same time! Causing blood to skeet and splatter all over me and Garcia and the other three White boys! We didn't stop. I snatched him over on his back and me and Garcia proceeded to stomp him out. I was A-town stomping him like the old dance! This melee caused a semi-race riot out there in the yard, the couple of white boys, who was with the big white boy, came to his rescue, attacking Garcia. One of them had a knife, about to stab Garcia in his neck, but I stabbed him in the top of his head, making him forget about his knife!

By this time, some more Aryan Brotherhood had bumrushed the show but, a lot of black guys had done joined in along with the Mexicans. When the dust cleared after the police came. It was a lot of bloody white boys. A few bloody blacks and Mexicans. A lot of people got away, but unfortunately, me and Garcia got ratted out and ended up in lock-up.

We were in cells next to each other in segregation. We communicated constantly through the vents and passing notes through a hall runner.

"Antonio, I like to thank you for helping me out in the yard. You saved my life!" Said Garcia.

"Ain't nuthin to it Amigo... You my potna!! I wasn't about to let that big ass cracka handle you!! What you about, 5'5" to 5'4", a hundred and fifty pounds soaking wet?"

"Ha-ha" Laughed Garcia, "Something like that. Hey... you

ain't much taller than me maan!! What you about 5'6" to 5'7"?"

"Yeah! I'm 5'7 weighing in at the ripped-up, buffed-up 207!!" I laughed at myself.

"Seriously speaking maan, I got something for you... Something for you when you get out!!" Said Garcia.

"What's up Garcia, talk to me," I asked Garcia.

"No-noo, Antonio! I'll put it on paper when the hall runner comes through...okay?" Said Garcia.

"Dat's what's up!"

"I'm going to sit down, and write it now... I got a feeling we will be shipped out of here soon, due to the authorities' fear of a riot. It's been locked down the last three days." Said Garcia.

"Okay, do yo thang Amigo, I'm about to lay back and think a lil bit," I said to Garcia.

"Do that Antonio! That's why I like you! Besides the fact, that you're loyal, you're a thinking man. Also, you'll execute your thoughts and plans!" Said Garcia.

"You know what to say!" I said.

Smiling to myself. BANG BANG BANG "What the fuck!" I yelled, jumping up out of my bed, dazed. I had done nodded off, thinking too hard.

"Antonio, there's the letter from your partner next door." It was the segregation's wing, Hall runner throwing Garcia's letter through the tray hole in the door.

"Okay... Good looking out." I told the runner, as I picked the letter up. It was sealed in an envelope, so I know this got to be deep. "Greeting Amigo! I stuck to my words and wrote this letter. As I told you we might be transferred soon... Very soon... The authorities fear a riot... It doesn't matter because we will communicate through our families. You saved my life and besides we're friends. So, to show you my appreciation for your loyalty and friendship, I got a blessing for you once you get out!! To clear the air. No... it's not a setup. I wouldn't do people like that! Death – Before – Dishonor! Here is my wife's address and phone number, Anita Abregado, 2160 Horshoe Bend Drive, Dallas Texas. Home phone #(213)776-8646 and cell #(610) 272-8567.

These numbers will never change amigo. Well, maybe the cell phone number but, not the home phone! Write me back A.S.A.P and give me your info. We will keep in touch, no matter what happens. Your friend, Garcia.

After I read Amigo's letter, I immediately wrote him back. While I was writing him back, he hollered at me through the vents, "Amigo, Amigo!!"

"Yeah Amigo, what's up?" I answered.

"Did you get the letter?"

"Yeah, I got it... And I'm writing you back right now!" I said.

"Good, good. Make sure you get it right back to me tonight when the runner comes through. He should be through here soon after the 10:30 count."

"Okay, Amigo, I got you."

"Oh yeah." Said Garcia. "Try to learn as much Spanish as you can. Order a book or get one from the prison library before you get out."

"Okay, Amigo." Just as soon as the runner came through, I stopped him and gave him the letter to pass to Amigo. He called me through the vents to let me know he got it.

"Amigo... what did I tell you?"

"What's that Amigo?" I asked.

"I just got word that we are leaving in the morning!" Said Amigo.

"For real."

"Yes... I don't know where to right now. But it's been affirmed, that we are leaving." And just as sure as Garcia said it the C.O.'s came around and got us and about 40 more inmates from lock up and population! Blacks, Whites, and Mexicans and split us up, and flew us in different directions, in the United States.

I, myself ended up at Coleman, U.S.P. In Florida, outside of Orlando. Garcia ended up in ADX, Florence. That's in Florence, Colorado. In the same prison was Larry Hoover. I stayed in lock up for close to two years, but the whole time, I was scheming and fighting my state murder case on my own, until I wrote my ex-lawyers, ex-wife, who in turn was a lawyer and she started working for me, for Free! Not at first though!

Once I got out of lock-up and ran into one of my homeys from my hood, Antone Capone, it was on! That nigga was hooked up with all the racket running folks and I got right in with him and was hustling, sending my family and my new lawyer what I could until we took our relationship to another level. Me and Garcia communicated regularly through letters through our families up until the day I got out.

And here I am now committing murder for hire for my Mexican partner! After about 3 days of being free, I called Ms. Anita Abregado, to tell her to pass the news to her husband that I was out, and I gave her my number. Garcia called me the same day. "Hey, my friend!" Said Garcia.

"What up Migo!"

"You've finally made it thank God!!"

"Yea migo, it's beautiful out here. I'm just chillin wit my fam!"

"That's good! I no mean to interrupt, just thought I would congratulate you!"

"Nawl, you cool Amigo! You my potna!" I said as I got up from the couch and went outside. "You need something? You know I got yo info."

"No Antonio, I'm good. Just want to pass on a little wisdom right now."

"Okay Amigo," I said knowing Garcia was about to sprinkle me with some game.

"Antonio... the time I've know you I came to the conclusion that you have plenty of potential, plenty of potential to get right like you want to be. And the quality of loyalty, to go with it, is going to carry you a long way. Just be careful of who you trust and deal with. Do you remember what I told you when we were in lock up?"

"Yea migo." I answered.

"Whenever you're ready, I'm willing to show you my appreciation for your friendship and loyalty."

"Shit Garcia, you already know what's up! Just give me a couple of months, to soak this shit in, and get used to being out, and learning what's, what, then we can go from there."

"Okay Antonio, whenever the time is right, call my wife. In fact, go to Dallas and meet her. She's very cool and anxious to meet you, but don't take anyone with you. She'll be your plug! And with that, I'll talk to you later."

"Okay Amigo, keep your head up."

"You do the same, Antonio."

After a couple of months of being out, I caught a flight from Montgomery, Alabama to Dallas, Texas to meet Anita. She met me once I got off the plane. She was driving a Range Rover. She took me to their mansion, where their son and two daughters were waiting. Their son was around 25 or 26. Cool as a fan loved to smoke weed and chase women. A playboy! The two daughters were twins, around the ages of 21 or 22. Beautiful and fine as fuck!

Introductions were made, and we sat down and talked as their personal chef served us dinner. On the low, I'm looking around amazed at their layout. Garcia was ballin! After dinner, we sat around, talked some more, and Garcia's kid offered to take me out on the town. Their family appreciated me rolling with Garcia in the pen and they showed me!

They took me shopping and spent about 10 grand on me! Clothes, shoes, and jewelry.

"My father extends his gratitude to you in a big way!"

"I thank ya'll too Renaldo!"

"No, we thank you for saving Pop's life!!"

I just nodded my head! "No problem," I said and that's when Renaldo came with it.

"Antonio, I know this may seem strange or it may not, but my father needs a favor."

"Okay, Renaldo, what's up?"

"We need his co-defendant knocked off... If not him, his son! His son would be the sacrifice for his father! A message!" Hissed Renaldo. "I already know that you know his situation... my father."

"Yeah... I know." I said, feeling kind of thrown, but

quickly recovered because this is what goes on in cartel business.

"My father stands a great chance of getting back in court. A new trial on appeal. And his codefendant doesn't need to make it. He will probably testify again.

Looking Renaldo in the eyes a couple of seconds before I answered him "Okay… When do you want this done?"

"Anytime… Just let me know when you're ready!" Answered Renaldo. "I know that you're just getting out… give yourself time." My father's lawyer is just in the process of filing his petition, but …"

"Give me 30 days, and I'll be ready." I interrupted.

Renaldo slowly nodded his head. "Okay, okay… 30 days it is." We've already had him under surveillance, we know his movements and all. When his son comes up missing this will draw him out! Like a moth to the flame!

Later on, that night Renaldo and his sisters took me out to some cool clubs. Even got me some Mexican pussy, which I enjoyed and thoroughly fucked. Fucked so good that she wanted to keep in touch! The next morning Renaldo came and picked me up at the hotel. "Mother wants to see and talk to you before you catch your flight." Renaldo was driving a Black Lambo. These Mexicans weren't bullshittin, they still had plenty of money! They made moves every now and then. Other than that, they ran businesses. Once we got to their mansion I was greeted by Anita, Garcia's wife, at the door.

"Heeey Antonio come on in! Did you have a nice time last night?

"Oh yeah, Anita!" I smiled, "one of the best nights of my life."

"Good, good! Come in and have brunch with us!" Said Anita. We sat down, ate, and drunk coffee afterward. "Come." Said Anita, as she rose from her chair, beckoning for me to come with her. I got up, and we walked out of the back-door, to an enormous patio. "Antonio it's obvious you know what type of business my husband is in."

"Right," I said, slowly nodding my head up and down.

"I was instructed by him to make sure you receive his gift from him in hopes that this will enhance our relationship. "Take a cab to this address." Said Anita, as she handed me an old receipt with the info on the back. "It will be a min-van there, occupied by two Mexican women in the driveway, there will be a Mercedes Benz S550. You will drive the Mercedes back to your town and the ladies will follow you. The lady's cellular number is here on this card." Said Anita, handing me a plain white card with a phone number on it. Just in case if you lose each other or something."

"What you want me to do with the Mercedes once I get back to Atlanta?" I asked Anita.

"Oh... That is part of your gift from my husband... It's paid for. "The Mexican ladies will leave the van with you and you will take them to the airport A.S.A.P we'll make arrangements, the next visit, to get the van back. Antonio, I hope that everything goes alright with you and the blessings from my husband." Said Anita, as she held eye contact with me, for a couple of seconds before I answered.

"It will Anita."

"I'm sure it will." Smiled Anita. "Once you get the mini-van, take heed to these instructions." Said Anita, as she handed me a note. "Then you'll find your gifts. The Madiwana is free of charge the mid-grade and the exotic. As for the Yayo, if the quality is high, nowadays, even with wholesale... 17-20... maybe 23, but as a gift from my husband 15 for you... You'll be able to do the math once you discover your gift." She stood there and looked me in my eyes for 5 long seconds, and then she spoke.

"Things will get better with time... especially once our problems are alleviated... The problems Renaldo spoke with you about."

"Yes... I know... 30 days." I said I was a little nervous, but for the numbers of these people talking, I quickly got my mind right. Renaldo came and got me, looking like some type of Flamboyant Latin Superstar. Anita hugged and kissed me before I left.

"Antonio... Take your time. Let us know if something goes wrong... But take your time." Said Anita.

"Okay, Anita... I got you and take care of yourself. I'll most definitely see you soon."

Renaldo took me to my hotel, to gather my things and I called a cab and directed the cab driver to the address Anita had written on the paper she gave me. About 10 minutes later the cabbie was dropping me off in another sprawling suburb of big mansions, and just like Anita said there were two Mexican women sitting in a blue dodge. One young, the other older like mother and daughter. We locked eyes only for a couple of seconds, as I walked to the midnight Blue S550 Mercedes Benz. I looked in the car and the keys were sitting on the seat.

"Damn, I hope I remember how to get to the interstate," I said to myself, as I got in the Benz and crunk up. Pulled up next to the minivan and asked the women how to get to the highway. They didn't say anything. They just crunk up and led the way up until we reached Interstate 20 and that's when I took the lead, non-stop to Louisiana. Stopping only to use the bathroom, all the way to Mississippi, Alabama, to sweet Georgia!!

Once we got to Atlanta to one of my bitches crib. I had already called a cab, so it was only 2 minutes, once we pulled up, the cab was there, and the minivan was in the garage. Door down and me in it following Anita's instructions.

"Hit the lights (3-times) hit the brakes (6 times) and Walla there go them Bricks!! And Pounds!! All kinds of secret compartments flipped open!! My heart was beating like a muthafucka. Just of sheer excitement. At first, it didn't look like much, until I grabbed the packages and felt how heavy they were. They were all gift wrapped and vacuum-sealed. I cut the first one open with a pocketknife that came with the pack! 10 Bricks all wrapped together with a scorpion in the middle of each Brick!

I grabbed the other two gift-wrapped packages which were both kinds of heavy and cut them open. "OOO-WOO! This some gas!" I said, after pulling a big bud off of the weed, I didn't have a scale right there at the time, but it felt like 2-50 pound bales of some good mid-grade weed. I opened the other gift, it was some Cush! 14 ½ pounds of some grandaddy and 14 ½ pounds of some California Orange Cush! Man, it's on!

Chapter 3

THE HIT & 30 DAYS LATER

It didn't take any time to flip the work! The quality of the yay was 98% with a good price of $25,000 per kilo. In the game now that's a great price! With all the bullshit dope with high prices, it had no choice but to fly! Quick flip! I profit a quick $10,000 with 10 of them and I got a quick 100 racks! I could've made more but, I thought like "Fuck it! Put this good product out here for the low niggaz gone jump on it. Put the whip game on it, make plenty of money, and come back and get some more!

Some niggaz was just going to make them quick juugs off of it. You know just play the middleman and charge anywhere from 26 to 30 grand and make them some money. Then come back and shop for themselves and make me rich... Quick! I didn't give a fuck because I had one motive and that was to be major paid!! All the pain and struggle me and my fam done been through there ain't no way I was going to just be mediocre or broke.

According to Forbes in the U.S. of A, if you only made $25,000 a year or lower you are considered poor. A million dollars a year or more you're considered rich! I wanted to be on that end. A million dollars a year or more. Rich!

As for the weed I dumped all that on about 4 or 5 of my cousins. A split between the ones in Georgia and Alabama for the low price of $500 an lb. for the mid and $2,000 a pound for the exotic. So that made me a quick hundred racks in weed money with $200 thousand, a gangsta plug. I can't lose! All I need is a loyal team!

Me and Chi-Chi, my partner from childhood, took a flight out to Texas. I already told Renaldo that I was bringing my partner with me because he's a loyal, standup guy and been down with me forever. Chi-Chi held me down through my bid up until he fell with some federal distribution charges. He got caught up with me on my murder case but, didn't shoot the victim he shot one of his partners. So, he got charged with an assault for that and did 2 years. He got out but, in the next 2 years, he caught the fed case and did about 8 years.

While in the joint he studied computer networking and programming. When he got out, he went to school and got degreed and certified. Now he's working for some big firm and married with kids. But, on the low just as dangerous and slick as me and down to make some quick juugs on some co-caine! Not to mention the stable of women.

I sold the first 10 bricks through Chi-Chi. One of my old school cousins and one of my partners is an Alabama implant in Atlanta Lil Dontay. I had already overnight mailed Anita her $150,000 and my money to re-up $150,000 plus stashed $50,000.

So, once me and Chi-Chi got to the airport in Dallas all we had to do was rent a car. A day before, I had already paid 2 college girls to drive the minivan to Shreve Port, Louisiana. Leave it at the Holiday Inn and Anita sent someone to retrieve it. We rented a Malibu and I called Anita to let her know we were there. We got a hotel suite downtown at the Sheraton and waited for Anita to call with more instructions and plans. It didn't take long because, within 10 minutes she called and told us to meet her in Cockrell Hill, a suburb southwest of Dallas not far from our hotel.

Once we arrived at this mansion, she directed us to her and Renaldo. I introduced her and Renaldo to Chi-Chi. After the pleasantries, we left Chi-Chi sitting under some shade trees with a mixed drink. We walked around and talked business. Renaldo was laying the outline of the plan to me.

"Like I told you on your last visit, we've had him under surveillance," said Renaldo, speaking on the turncoat Carlos Desendez. "He has been in the witness protection program since the traitor ratted my father out. We located him through some of our people who got people in the F.B.I. He's living under the alias Juan Vasquez out in Montana but, he takes regular trips back to Mexico to visit his son in Guadalajara. His son goes to college there." said Renaldo as he pulled a picture of Desendez's son out of his pocket.

I looked at the picture and studied it for about 60 seconds. Then I handed it back. He must've read my mind because he said "I know a lot of us look alike but don't worry. We'll make sure you get the right one!" That's when he pulled out another photo of a special edition Z6 Corvette, two-toned black and red. "His father was upset about his son's lack of judgment with being flamboyant." He pulled out another picture and handed it to me. It was an apartment complex. "This is where he lives in Guadalajara." His father is very slippery, but his son isn't. Matter of fact, they're not even suspecting a hit!"

"They're fairly comfortable now, but his father is still kind of skeptical. Don't worry... once we go to Mexico we'll show you and your friend everything!"

"Let me ask you this Renaldo... Why haven't they been hit?" I asked.

"It's only a few my father trust for one... And second, your loyalty and ruthlessness won my father's trust in this type of work. It's like you're making your bones with the cartel... We'll make sure you're well taken care of! Rich for life!"

I smiled at that not knowing if it was game or what... but fuck it I'm all in!! "Well... when is it going down?" I asked.

"Soon." Said Renaldo. No later than a day or two from now." "We'll take off for Mexico in the next 30 minutes."

"Antonio, I received the money... that was fast!" Smiled Anita.

"Umma try to be fast all the time!" I said.

"No, don't rush it if you don't have to. Take your time. Once ya'll come back from Mexico I'll have directions for you to pick up your other vans."

"Damn! Vans as in plural?" I was thinking to myself. Once me and Anita got through discussing business. We followed Renaldo to a rental car, got in, and pulled off.

Renaldo already had some fake passports, fake ID, and the works. We rented another car in Dallas and followed Renaldo all the way to the border in San Luis, Mexico. Once we made it through the checkpoint we stopped for some gas and knick-knacks and headed on to Benjamin Hill. We left the rentals with some of Renaldo's family and caught a private plane to Guadalajara. Renaldo had some cars already on deck. We took them to this hotel and checked in.

Renaldo threw a bag of some good exotic weed on the table along with some cigarillos. He pulled out his iPhone and started speaking in Spanish as he walked off.

Me and Chi-Chi proceeded to break down cigarillos rollin up and lighting up! Renaldo came and smoked with us as he was finishing his conversation. "That was our people who has Desendez son under surveillance." "They've learned his predictable movements. Come... let me show you around," said Renaldo walking to the door.

We got up and followed him out the door. For an hour and a half, Renaldo was showing us the whole city of Guadalajara, along with spots the son of Carlos Desendez frequented. They even had the times that he had classes at the University.

"Give us a full day. Let's say tomorrow... to put him under our own surveillance to match up with your people's surveillance... we'll have him! He'll be in heaven in 48 hrs." I said.

"Good, good." Said Renaldo.

The next day me and Chi-Chi were up early sitting outside of Carlos Jr.'s girlfriend's apartment. We were going to follow him all day and night to map out a nice spot to knap or whack him. We had already ridden to a desolate area in the desert outside of Tiaque Paque and dug a shallow grave. We were concealed by the tint on the windows of the old white Tahoe we were driving. We were strapped up with 2 AR 15's, a taser, a .45, and a .44 Bulldog. The taser was for kidnapping purposes. If we get close enough, hit him with the taser, nap him quickly and take him to his grave. We sat there 2 ½ hours before he came out as scheduled.

We followed him to the college where he practically hung out all day. We trailed him later that evening to a couple of his hangouts, including this bar which was the perfect spot to snatch him and that's what we did.

Fuck the next day! Carlos Jr. pulled up to his favorite bar and stopped in a dark spot. Me and Chi-Chi pulled right up next to him in the parking lot. Could've shot him right there and left him in the Vette but, my potna Garcia wanted it to be a heartfelt message to his ex-partner.

As soon as we pulled up, Carlos Jr. was exiting his whip and we were too. He was kind of startled by the sudden opening of the doors to the Tahoe, but being the careless person he is, he ignored us, and that's when Chi-Chi hit him with the taser! Enough to knock him to the ground. Once he hit the ground, I was all over him cuffing him like the police, snatching him up and throwing him in the back seat of the Tahoe.

Before he could mumble a word, I knocked him out with the .44 Bulldog. At that time Chi-Chi was pulling off and I was in the back seat going through his pockets with the gloves on. This fool wasn't even strapped! He drove to the spot in Tiaque Paque.

"Get yo ass up!" I said as I was slapping him awake, and throwing him out of the truck on his face.

He tried to roll over as he was mumbling in Spanish. "Irre...incredible, unreal, unbelievable." Said Carlos Jr.

"Oh, it's real," I said as I went through his phone trying to find his father's number.

Garcia was right about learning a little Spanish, cause I would be halfway lost now! Easy find though. It was in his contacts under "Papi". I took a pic of Carlos Jr. as he stood in front of his own shallow grave with his head bleeding. Crying and asking, "What did I do?" In English.

Right after I sent the picture to Carlos Sr., he answered on the first ring. "Hola!" "I have your moCO'so (brat) and don't bullshit, I know that you know English mufucka!" A long silence on the other end. "Ay-Amigo ya hear me?" "I know you got the pic I sent you. I'm gonna send you another one after this." BOOM BOOM BOOM BOOM Echoes the .44 Bulldog.

"Nooooooooooo!" Hollered Carlos Sr. through the phone. In agony cause, he knows what just happened. I done shot a video of his son being gunned down. As he fell in the shallow grave, I stood over him and finished him off. "BOOM". One more shot to the head.

"This is a message... don't ever show back up to court." And I hung the phone up. "Cover him up Chi-Chi." I said as I grabbed a shovel and started covering Carlos Jr. up. On the other end, Carlos Desendez Sr. was in shock. Still holding his phone after hearing the gunshots, after looking at the picture of his son, beat up, standing with his hands behinds his back... Crying!

Finally, he opened the video, which was sent to him from his son's phone.

"Por-Favor! Por-Favor!" BOOM BOOM BOOM BOOM... BOOM BOOM

These were his son's last words and the pistol going off. He dropped his phone and stood there in a daze. Thinking about the call he got from this Black man, "Don't ever show back up to court." Then the gunshots!... He knew what had happened. He was paying dearly for his sins. The crime he committed against one of his best friends, Garcia Abregado. He was standing there still in a daze when his phone rang! Snapping out of his daze he grabbed the phone off the floor and looked at the caller ID. It was from his dead son's phone.

"Hola," Said Carlos.

"Hola to you too! Look... We'll snatch a family member a month to let you know I ain't playing!"

"Who are you?! Who are you working for?!" Said Carlos.

"Just don't go to court!!" I said and hung up.

Carlos sat there looking at his phone. He sat down in his Lazyboy and cried like a baby.

I threw the phone in the Big Lake Inocotian along with the .44 Bulldog on the way back to Guadalajara. I called Renaldo from my throw-away phone to let him know the news.

"Hello." Answered Renaldo.

"It's done."

Renaldo paused for a couple of seconds before answering "Already?!... I thought you was going to wait 'til tomorrow?"

"Change of plans... It was too sweet to pass up! He landed right in my arms. I'm headed back to the hotel. Should be there in 5 minutes."

"I'm on my way!" Said Renaldo.

We got back to the hotel and Renaldo was pulling right in at the same time. We sat down and smoked a couple of cigarillos and told Renaldo what happened. Holding back no details. I had forwarded the photos and video from Carlos Jr.'s phone to my throwaway and shared it with Renaldo.

"Perfect!" Said Renaldo as he handed my phone back to me. We left the hotel that same night and made it to the private airplane. Then we flew back to San Luis and spent the night. Woke up early the next morning and headed back across the border then straight to Dallas, Texas.

Chapter 4

(FROM DALLAS TO ATLANTA)

Anita was elated about the news, "Gracias Antonio!" said Anita hugging me and kissing me on my cheeks. "Now my husband stands a great chance of getting out!"

"Carlos should've got the message Anita." I said.

"Let's get back to our other business." Said Anita. Barely blinking an eye. "For the $150,000 we gave you 10 kilos and another 10 on consignment. Don't worry about the madiwana. For the work you just put in for us we're giving you 500 lbs. of popcorn mid and 100 lbs. of cush on co-signment, for $80,000. That's 3 vehicles headed to Atlanta!"

I couldn't do nothing but smile! 3 vans of contraband headed to the A! "Can't do nothing but get rich now." Is what I'm saying to myself. Let me get this shit straight with Anita. "Okay Anita... question. For the cleanup job you're paying me 500 lbs. of popcorn?"

"Yes... oh those are yours free of charge. And the cush when you come back." Said Anita. "Oh yeah... If you're going to continue doing business with us call this number. If you don't get an answer, they'll call you back... a female... give her your code number-name." That's when Anita handed me a piece of paper. I opened it up and there it was "I-C Note".

"She will hang up, that's when you text your order to her like the instructions on the paper."

I looked at the paper again and that's when I saw it. Example: For 10 bricks, say "I put 10 stamps on it, on the box." If you want the popcorn, continue to text, "For $100 shoes. For more "For the $100 shoes, 5 pair" 500 lbs. Then for the exotic say "Louboutins shoes. 1-pair-100 lbs. etc."

After I read it, I'm like damn, they got this shit by the hundreds!!

"You understand Antonio?" Asked Anita.

"Yeah, I got it locked in my mind."

"Good!" Said Anita. Anita stepped to me and hugged me one more time. "Once again... Thanks, Antonio. Garcia is very happy! He already has the news. He said he will give you a call in the near future."

"Okay!" I said.

"You do remember how to get to Cockrell Hill?" Asked Anita.

"Yes," I said.

"That's where you'll be driving that too," said Anita pointing at a brand new black 2021 Range Rover.

"Okay... what you want me to leave there and switch up or something?" I asked Anita. She smiled. "No, that's another gift from my husband!" I'm like "Whoa, Whoa... I mean. I appreciate it... but."

"No, no take it. It's yours!" said Anita.

I had almost forgotten that when these types of people give you a gift and you don't take it. They look at that situation as if you're dissing them. "Okay Anita, I'll take it. I appreciate it."

"Don't worry about it... we own a couple of dealerships." Smiled Anita.

These folks, mega-rich, and I'm trippin! The keys were already in the ignition. Me and Chi-Chi jumped in the truck and headed out to the hotel to get our belongings. We left the hotel in 5 minutes flat and drove over to Cockrell Hill. Just like Anita said there were 3 vehicles waiting. A minivan, Suburban, and Yukon Denali. They were up on a big wrecker truck and 2 Mexican men were driving the truck with nothing more than a nod of their heads in greeting. We were off to the races to Interstate 20 with no problem. We made it back to Atlanta with the vehicles unloaded at another spot.

Once we put all the workup. I took Chi-Chi home and went home to my new spot. A condo downtown and laid down trying to go to sleep. But doing numbers in my head was keeping me awake staring at the ceiling.

Chapter 5

(LAYING DOWN THE FOUNDATION)

After 2 hrs. of lying there tossing and turning and anticipating. I finally fell asleep... dreaming like a mufucka! 18 wheelers full of cocaine, weed, heroin and all type of drugs was getting unloaded by me, Chi-Chi, couple of more niggaz and some Mexicans. Then suddenly all kinds of lights, sirens, and flash bombs were going off. That's when I jumped out of my sleep.

"Shit!" I said, wiping sweat off of my face. Federal nightmares! Fucking anxiety or something got me in a state of, insomnia. I got up, fixed myself a Ciroc on the rocks, rolled a blunt of cush and flipped on the TV. It was on a video station and they were playing some of the old Jeezy.

"Cauze um a Rida! (Yeaaah!) Um, a sole survivor!" It seemed as if the song was talking to me!

I was in a slight trance from the weed and alcohol, but more so from what I got myself involved in! This was some deep shit! I mean... I grew up in the game and left the streets somewhat deep in the game on a smaller scale. Now I'm plug-life, knee-deep in the game, and when it's time to re-up. I'm knee-deep in the caine! Like the song is talking to the depths of my soul! I done lost so many niggaz to this game. Family members and all! So, I should really be squared up with a job! But, in my world to be squared up means to be broke or barely getting by. It means to be ordinary and that's hard to be when you've never been an ordinary nigga! To be out of the trenches makes you hungry! Makes me so obsessed with this money-making that there's nothing I really fear! My ambition is to be boss!

"You ain't never seen Dem pies, talking so much white it can hurt yo eyes." (Yeah!) I really lived it man," the Jeezy is on blast on my surround sounds as I get up to take a shower. Since I'm up and in a zone, I'm ready to get it!

I'm out early this morning creeping in a rental and peeping the scene because I just left the stash spot. Been fuckin with the work! It is some money on my hustling phone now! Got a couple of Alabama niggaz coming through for the white girl, mid and loud!! I haven't put any whip on it yet! Selling it just like it is straight-drop cocaine! They can take it and shit on it all they want! Good cocaine going to bring them out! Chi Chi is going to help me with the corporate legal side of the business and right now I'm holding the streets down! I'm going to have to fuck with some street niggaz I know and decipher from there who to make my lieutenants. At least 2 loyal real-ass niggaz who's hungry and ready to stack some paper on a big level! Someone with the wits and nuts to handle thangz. Niggaz that know how to peep fake, snake niggaz! A hard task!

I had been hollering at a childhood friend from the 4th ward Sonny when I first got the plug and the work. So, I was already working a lil through him back in the days he was on, but at the same time, he had a rep as a young Jackboy. Oh...

and love to slang the iron! So, a few people might be scared to do business with him. Nevertheless, he's still known and relevant on East Blvd and abroad. After serving the Alabama dudes a couple of bricks and pounds I stashed the paper in another empty townhouse then I called Sonny.

"What's up nigga?" I asked.

"What's up Bru?!" Said Sonny.

"Where you at?"

"I'm over my baby mama's house!"

"Damn nigga which one?!" I asked. Sonny had plenty of baby mama's.

"I'm over in the Bluff."

"Okay, I'm coming in your direction! Be there in 10 minutes."

"Bet!" Said Sonny and hung up.

Once I got over there, I lit me up a blunt from the new weed I had brought from Texas.

"Damn! What the fuck is that?!" asked Lamont, Sonny's oldest son.

"Here try it," I said as I passed the blunt. I know he's going to like it and going want some of it to hustle! Even though in this area the primary product is heroin. I know good weed going to sell everywhere! Sonny's son is a hustla like him so I can build some clientele through him. Especially, when I get that Jackie Chan! The heroin!

"So, what's going on Antonio?!" said Sonny, ready to get down to business.

"Going price still the same?" I asked Sonny. Referring to the prices of the bricks of coke on the streets now.

"Still the same! High as fuck! But I got some people ready to spend on that fire you had!"

"Dats wusup!" "Well, check this out... nigga um da plug from here on out!" Sonny likes this type of talk! He was smiling like Chester the Cheetah, as he cleaned his Mac-90. I briefly filled him in on what's about to take place as I smoked with his son. Sonny don't smoke or drink! All he does is drink juices, fuck plenty of women, and get money! "I got something for you too Lamont! But for now, I'm just going to dump some of this same weed we smoking right now on you. Can you handle it?!"

Lamont smirked at the question. "Try me!" said Lamont. I smiled at that cause I can see the hunger in his eyes.

"Okay... give me your number and I'll get back in touch later today."

"Bet!" Said Lamont. Then he gave me his number and I called him.

"Lock that in," I said referring to my number. As me and Lamont were discussing business about the weed and so forth Sonny's phone vibrated.

"Hello?!" Answered Sonny, as he walked off.

"How much can you handle?" I asked Lamont. "I'm talking in pounds maybe bales!"

"Shit! How much can you give me?!"

I looked into his eyes and studied him a moment before answering him. "I'll give you a 50 lb. bale... for starters. Can you handle that?"

He smiled. "4-Sho!" said Lamont. "What I'm going to owe you?"

I already knew that the going rate on a pound in the A

was $8-900, so I'm about to let him see his self. "Give me 20 racks!!" I can see he was doing the math in his head before he answered.

"Bet!" said Lamont as he shook my hand.

"Oh yeah... It won't be long, I'll be having Boy! I know that's what y'all moving over here pretty heavy!"

"You already know!" said Lamont.

"I got you," I said as Sonny came back into the living room.

"Ay. I got some people ready now! What's up? Between 3 niggas 7 bricks!" Said Sonny.

"I'll get wit you," I said as I got up and hit the door. Just like clockwork I went and got the work for Sonny from my spot where I had the 10 bricks hid. Met him at this white chic's crib I fuck wit and gave him the whole 10 piece! The seven he was juuging to the folks and 3 on his face. I made $175 racks out of the 7. Ain't no telling what he made! I had grabbed a 50 lb. bale of mid for Lamont, took it to another white chic's crib I met in Club Cheetah's, and swiftly got that bale to him. I wasn't bullshittin so I got with my old-school cousin and moved 5-bricks through him to some niggaz out of South Carolina. Along with half of the other 50 lb. bale and 5lbs. of cush. The other 15 lbs. of cush I dumped on my homey Dontay an Alabama implant. He bought half and I fronted the other half. The only thing I had left was 400 more pounds of the midgie and 90 lbs. of cush. It's time to head back down to Texas!

Chapter 6

(BUILDING THE HOUSE)

Later that night I was on a red-eye flight to Dallas, Texas, full speed ahead! I had texted my order to Anita's people that were on stand-by and sent my money earlier that day! Chi-Chi didn't even know I was gone! I wasn't bullshittin! I sent them $150,000 for 10-blocks of Yay (cocaine). She fronted me plus $300,000 for some more blow. That's 20 keys! I know she's going to front me 20 more to go along with that! I still owed them 200 racks for the cush but, they're not worried about that. I'll start dumping all the mid and cush on Lamont, Dontay, my cousin, and Lil One in Alabama. 2 of my cousins in the A, Jazzy and his brother Lin, and some on one of my lil niggaz... Brainhead! This lil nigga was an official shooter! I met him in the state prison in Alabama. Brainhead was a young nigga who went to school with my daughter. He got caught up in some robbery-kidnap-attempted murder shit in Alabama. He got out before me and was back in Atlanta doing his thang with the loud and mid. He was doing okay but just needed that major push which I was going to do later.

Upon arrival, I was greeted at the airport by one of Anita's drivers/goons she used when she wanted to be chauffeured around in her stretch Lincoln Limo. Nothing more than a head nod between the driver and I as he opened the back door for me.

"Antonio!" Said Anita as she hugged me.

"Hey, Anita! How are you?!"

"I can't complain!" Said Anita as she raised the partition between us and the driver.

"How was your trip?" asked Anita.

"Got a lil jet lag, but um okay."

"Let's talk business," said Anita.

"I should get the money today... shortly. I see what you paid for and ordered. I'm going to go ahead and give you a total of 50 for that."

My mind was running like a hellcat charger now! She's talking 50 bricks! I'm doing the math in my head, and that's $750,000 with me paying her $450,000 that's $300,000 profit for me! I'm going to move them pretty quickly, so I'll be a millionaire in no time!

"Is that cool Antonio? Can you handle it?"

"Oh yeah, Anita! I was just doing some math in my head."

Anita laughed at that and placed her hand on mine, "Antonio... It's going to get better. I promise you! You'll be a multimillionaire in no time. You must stick with us and make the right decisions on your end with your money and the people you deal with. I suggest you make plans on cleaning your money up and making it legit! Because you're going to make lots of it."

"You're right!" I said to Anita. With my imagination, drive, and hustle I was destined to be a major!

Chapter 7

(1 YR. LATER)

"Bitch ass nigga! Where dat money at?!" Said Brainhead as he tortured these two delinquent niggaz. Not delinquent in the sense of being a juvenile, but in the sense of being late with my check!! It had been 4 months since I hit them off with the work! A total of 10 keys! "So y'all niggaz think um playing or something?" Asked Brainhead as he stood behind the two.

We had them out on the Chattahoochee River in a boat, in the dark, on their stomach hogtied and hanging off the side of the boat.

"Bru... we know you ain't playing! Give us two weeks! I swear I'll have the money Antonio talk to this young nigga! Please!" Hollered Brad, as he tried to convince me to speak up. Brad was the main one between the 2 because I was fucking with him first. The other nigga was his cousin that I met through Brad. I met Brad through his cousin Kadia who I met on Facebook 4 years earlier when I was in the pen playing with cell phones. 7 months after being released I reconnected with Kadia and started hooking up with her every weekend. She was right there in Columbia, South Carolina so it was nothing to jump on the slab and go see bout this fine K-Michelle-built woman. She was older than she looked! She had the body of a

24-year-old stripper, but she was 36! I had started fucking her and smoking cush with her on the regular learning about their streets and drug trade. Kadia was a hip bitch who fucked with hustlers.

Just so happen her cousin Brad was pushing blow. He was doing okay copping a quarter of brick here and there and by that time I had 50 bricks, so I put him on. I was in the process of expanding so I was fucking with out-of-towners. I had been letting him get by with a lot of bullshit on the strength of his cousin. I would never tell her none of our business, so she had no idea that he'd been fucking me around. I don't think he even knew he was fucking me around! Coming up short on the money constantly! Sob stories on how the dope came up missing. All type of shit! I felt like, he might've thought that I was soft or something due to my quiet demeanor. When that happens, a nigga will play you soft and surely try to take everything!

So, when I felt the rob-vibes coming from him, I immediately acted! I could tell he was on some setup-type shit when he called me to let me know that he was ready for some more work. I didn't even question him about the other money he owed me.

"Okay, give me a couple of hours and I'll be back with you. Want to come on to the A?"

"I'm going to put you all the way in the game," I said, hoping that his greed would take over.

"Uh... nawl, I'd rather for you to do like you been doing. You know you're straight in Columbia my nigga!" said Brad. He thought he was setting me up and all the time I'm setting him up! I already had a young nigga who be fronting and selling blow to ready to sell him out for bullshittin him! The youngster's name was Ricardo. Brad had been selling the dude whipped up ass dope, which wasn't coming back right. Fronting him the same bullshit and be expecting his money on time. He was stunting on Ricardo, in front of people trying to put some pimp shit down on Ricardo! I learned all this info through some pillow talk from another bitch named Shannon.

I reached out to him through her. It's amazing what an 8th of a key and a good strong plug could do! I kicked it with Ricardo at a strip club in Columbia, South Carolina. I let him know who I was. Brad's plug! And if he started doing business with me that I would make him stronger than Brad! I would make him a star! Under one condition at that moment and that was to learn Brad's movements and when is a good moment to catch him by himself.

When I brought the proposition to the youngster, I saw a devilish gleam in his eyes and a sheisty smirk on his face. "That's easy! I could do that!" Just like that, we were on Brad's ass! A couple of days prior to my meeting with Brad to sell him some work. Ricardo had been cold trailing him, learning his basic routine and when he's alone!

So, the day before I called him, Brainhead, Lansky, and Mandigo were in town. Posted up incognito! Riding low key, retracing the routine, to see where we would kidnap him. The day I made the call to Brad it was early in the morning. I had Lansky and Mandigo on stakeout close to Brad's house. Once I called him and told him I was ready he was on the move. Mandigo called me and told me they were on him and he was headed right in my direction towards his side chic's crib. That was cool because she was gone to work.

"Ay man, look like da nigga talking on the phone!" Said Mandigo.

"Okay... keep ya eyes open! How far is he from us?"

"He's maybe about... 5 minutes away." Said Mandigo.

"Okay... stay on him," I said as I ended the call. I grabbed my throwaway and called Brad. "Yo, hit me when you ready!" I said.

"Okay, okay... umm... I'll get back with you in 15 minutes," said Brad.

"No... make that 3 minutes I'm on the move Bru!" sounding as if I was in rush mode. "Aye, let me get back at you!" I said, interrupting Brad and hanging up. I wanted to time him just right. The element of surprise is very powerful. I was about 3 minutes late Brad was entering his side chic's neighborhood and that's when I called him. He didn't answer the phone.

At the same time, Mandigo was calling me. "Look like he on the phone!" Said Mandigo.

I don't know if he's feeling something funny and is calling up reinforcements or what, but I'm ready! As he turned on the street which led to his side chic's crib. I spotted another familiar car coming from the other end of the block. It was Brad's cousin.

He was in a red challenger and Brad was in a black one. We were on the side of the road acting as land surveyors. We were strategically placed. We were in a van with fake plates and fake business decals on the side of the van with work uniforms and hats. The van was parked out by the curb, in the road, in between the side-chick's crib and another house. Brainhead was on the other side of the driveway with a telescope-looking gadget. Looking through it as if he were actually surveying the land with his hard hat on. He looked professional. Me, I was at the van with the doors open.

Brad was pulling in kind of hesitant like he was suspicious as if we were the feds, but he turned on in the driveway. That's when I called him. He didn't answer. He grabbed the phone and looked at it and exited the car.

At that same time, his cousin pulled in. An unexpected catalyst to our plans but, we had a plan B in effect just in case this type of thing happened. It all happened so fast Brad nor his cousin knew what hit them! I chirped Brainhead from a walkie-talkie. "Ay watch my back, cover that nigga who just pulled up!" That's all it took and Brainhead was drawing iron!

"Don't move nigga! Get the fuck out of the car!!" said Brainhead.

"Oh Brad, you ain't answering the phone!" I said at the same time with 2 guns discreetly pointed at Brad's stomach trying not to draw attention from nosey neighbors. But we had already scoped it out, they're mostly gone to work.

"Damn Antonio, what's up man?!" Asked Brad as I quickly approached.

"This!" I answered as I shot him in the stomach with the taser gun and quickly cuffed him like the law!

"Ay man! What the fu..." By now, I'm duck taping his mouth and toting him to the van and Brainhead was doing the same to Brad's cousin after tasing him. We coming to see niggaz! We already had it understood to keep this shit quiet as possible. No blasting pistols unless necessary.

That's why I had Mandigo and Lansky playing the cold trailing position because they shoot quick as hell! They were just creepin by as we were stuffing Brad and his cousin in our fake work van.

"Brainhead drive!" I said as I threw him the keys. I stayed in the back with our captives. I rolled Brad over and snatched the duct tape off his mouth. "Nigga! Where my money at?!" I said.

"Damn, Antonio maan! You know I got you, I just been going through some shit!" Said Brad.

I knew this was a lie because the young nigga Ricardo had already put me on to game. On how the nigga hustling up there. And to confirm that his cousin Kadia had begun to talk a lil too much on how the lame was balling...! With my shit! And owed me!

Like that old Scarface saying... "Pay me my shit nigga! Pay me my shit!" That's the vibe I was on! "Nigga!" I said before cocking the Desert Eagle. "Take me to my shiit nigga!!" Amping my voice up for extra effects.

"Swear my nigga let me make some calls!" I swear I'll get the cake up..." "Augh!" Screamed Brad's cousin as I kicked him in his mouth.

"Lying ass nigga!! Aye, gone head to G.A. Brainhead. Teach niggaz a lesson bout crossing me!"

A couple of hours later, we're out on the boat in a dark part of the Chattahoochee River. I grew up fishing up and down the Chattahoochee in which runs from Atlanta down through South West Georgia. The Chattahoochee has history and was made infamous in the early '80s when 28 black children and a couple of adults came up missing and some of the victims were found dead in the river in Atlanta. Truth be told, ain't no telling how many corpses have been dumped in the Chattahoochee River from Atlanta all the way to Columbus, Georgia or the West Point dam! 2 is about to be added.

"Antonio talk to this young nigga... Please!" Hollered Brad.

"Dump him again!" I said. We were dumping these dudes slowly head-first into the dark river. Then holding them underwater for about 30 seconds before bringing them up for air and questioning them about my money! Making them think that they may just live which was a lie! Had to make some examples every now and then. The chastisement for the game! The word will get out that they've come up missing and people will know not to be fucking with me and mine. "Umma ask you one more time nigga... where my shit?!"

"COUGH COUGH CHOKE" Water was coming all out of Brad's mouth, nose, and everywhere. "Antonio (cough)... (cough)...(choke) Please! Man, I got... fuck (choke) I don't have all of it... my momma got..." Just as Brad was about to talk, I shot him in his stomach 3 times.

"Dump him and cut the rope!" I had already put a 50 lb. bag of cement mix on his back and on his cousin's back. It would be a while before they floated back to the surface. By then catfish, snakes, and all types of shit would be done eating them up and would be crawling all through their corpses! I wanted Brad to suffer a little going down to the bottom. That's why I gave him the stomach shots. His cousin... I shot him in his head. After making sure they both sank we took off.

Chapter 8

The game had escalated for me; within the year that I had been out. I was moving, supplying, and distributing cocaine, heroin, and weed up and down the Eastern seaboard! From Virginia, The Carolinas, Georgia, Northern Florida. Then over to Alabama parts of Tennessee and some in Jackson Mississippi! Atlanta was my home and base of operations. My Amigo and his wife had me and my crew eating like some kings. When Anita told me a year prior that she would make me a multimillionaire she wasn't lying. I was headed that way! As she had advised me to clean my money up. I got into some real estate and a trucking company called logistics.

First one of my cousins from Alabama, Bay-Ski had got a couple of 18 wheelers in the late '90s and was driving one of them. After getting his C.D.L. when he got out in 2003. He was later shot... murdered by a young nigga in 2009. So, I vowed to continue the business and keep his legacy going under a different name. "Deangelo's Transportation" Except I wasn't going to drive one. I would pay some people with C.D.L. licenses to do that! With all this product I'm getting from my plug, I need the trucks!

I met this white boy in prison name Paul. He had a degree

in logistics from Auburn University. By him knowing the warehousing logistic business I let him run the business but, I'm still hands-on! By now, I'm getting my dope by the pallets!! I'm learning the logistics business through Paul and on my own!

A year ago, after having that talk with Anita in her limo, making me a "multi-millionaire" conversation made me move that work quick as fuck and made me stack my paper fast and high! I remembered what this Jamaican nigga told me in the Summer of 1991. At Kilby Correctional Facility Receiving.

"If you g-wanna go back to de streets and hustle, get midget money!" Said Jamaica as he raised his hands up to his waist, describing a midget height. "Mwoney stacked up to here literally!" And that's what I was doing!

I had a stash of a lil over 1.6 million dollars in cash! And shit had just started to pop good. I wasn't buying shit hardly! I was still living in my condo downtown and at my girl's crib out in Lithonia and driving the Benz S550 and the Range Rover that Anita gave me. I did splurge on some rims and paint on my whips and stayed fresh to death and lil jewelry. I went to the clubs every now and then, but I wasn't making it rain. I was taking it to the banks and stash houses!

Family was mandatory! I moved my mother and both of my sisters into some nice houses in some nice neighborhoods. After the move with the 50 bricks, shit had got super turned up now! I got a team now and I'm the quarterback!

I was like Jeezy said "Mr. Reeing up wit bout 2 phantoms yea that's me okay." I was going back to re-up with a whole mil-ticket. A whole million dollars cash! Except, I wasn't sending it out there I was riding with it. In one of Anita's special made minivans. I had one of my old school homegirls, Vita with me. Looking like me and my Auntie or mother are on a trip or something. The price had done went down to 10 a key.

So, with the million I was copping a hundred of them and they were fronting a hundred for a milli! 200 bricks were going to be in my possession... Just like that! Anita even threw 5 bricks of high-grade heroin.

"Try it out, Antonio! I think you a good enough business-man to move it. Take your time with it!" She wanted back $500,000 for it. By now Anita had done set up a couple of restaurants and farmer markets in Atlanta. So, I didn't have to be worrying about getting the work back, etc. They had it loaded on 18 wheelers headed straight to the restaurants and farmer markets. I would go there in a 10-wheeler and load up! My distribution network had done grown limbs! I had to get a farm spot out in the country for some of my main captains, lieutenants, and customers to come to get the work! It wasn't many only a chosen few.

My partner Chi-Chi would come out there and get bout 20 bricks in which would hold his customers and hustlers down for a couple of weeks. He was chilling, doing his cor-porate thang. Living a family life and feeding some neighbor-hoods and small towns on the low! Sonny and his son would come out and score.

By now Sonny and his son, Lamont was getting money hard! I was dumping 40 bricks on Sonny in which he was flip-ping in a month. And his son was handling heroin and loud out in the Bluff. Once I saw he was a true-go-getter and a gangsta wit-it, I just drop a block of Boy on him along with 50 lbs. of mid and 50 lbs. of loud. My other partners Lil Dontay, his brother, my old school cousin.

They were getting yayo, mid and loud! Between the 3, that was 40 blocks, 200 lbs. of mid, and 75 lbs. of exotic weed. My other two cousins in the A, Jazzy and Lin were straight weed niggaz! Between the 2, that was 800 pounds of mid and 400 lbs. of loud. So, that left me with 100 blocks of fire cocaine to work with, 950 more pounds of mid, 425 lbs. of cush, and a couple of blocks of heroin! A couple of cats from Alabama were coming through shopping and I was fuckin with them heavy!

My partner Fat from Birmingham was getting half of the boy from me. About 2 ½ kilos of heroin. That was $250,000 coming from him monthly. My nigga Kindred was coming from Birmingham was getting 10 keys of cocaine a week. I'm selling them to him for 20 thousand apiece. That's 200K a week for me. 800 thousand a month! I got some fam in Anniston, Alabama area getting 10 keys along with 200 pounds every 2 weeks and I front him 10 more keys with them. So that's 40 a month gone through him. 800k a month there for me! 2 niggaz I knew from Montgomery had started getting 5 piece kilos of cocaine.

My partner Jack out of Brownville Community in Bama was getting 5 bricks of coke. My cuz Lil One in Opelika was getting 3 bricks of cocaine and 250 lbs. of midgie, and 100 lbs. of loud. And my cousin in Talladega, stay real was getting 2 bricks of coke, 100 lbs. of midgie, and 25 lbs. of exotic weed. That left me 300 lbs. of midgie and 300 lbs. of loud. I was shooting 100 lbs. of midgie to a chic I been knowing named Shelly over in Mississippi. Letting her split that with her cousin Christy who be everywhere between Atlanta, Opelika, Alabama, and Tuscaloosa, AL. The 200 lbs. of midgie and 300 lbs. of loud was dumped on Brainhead and he was hustling and feeding his goons with that! And acting the fuck up!!

Part 2

Any organization, criminal, etc. needs to be very well-funded, very well armed, very well organized, very well self-contained and very loyal!!

-Corey Bryant

Chapter 9

"Yeah, Yeah, Yeah!! Nigga I heard dat! But you need to come on and turn something in!" Said Brainhead in his signature rapid flow.

"Turn something in?" Asked the voice on the other end of the phone.

"Is all dat money there?!" Said Brainhead to a hustler who was shopping with him at the same time. The money was in different stacks in front of Brainhead on a picnic table. This nigga was in the park damn near open air-trapping like in the late '80s and early '90s on the block! Button-down Versace shirt, wide-open, flexing his chest, chains, and 2 pistols!

"Yeah, it's all there!" Said the customer as he nervously looked around at Brainhead's goons, which were high and flexin their iron in some form or fashion. All 3 of them clutchin! Brainhead was already turned up naturally and a nigga pulled up in the park, in front of me bumping that Eldorado red (out of Montgomery) and you Gotti.

"It's a concrete jungle! With lions, tigers, and bears." Rapped Brainhead, reciting the lyrics to the songs as he threw the grocery bag on the table and bounced around. Then somebody in another car was bumping "War-ready" by Rick

Ross and Jeezy. He sho-nuff turned up then! Front-line when you're war-ready just another hom-i-cide! When you're war ready!

"That's how you got to be my nigga!" Said Brainhead as he bobbed his head like a rock star and clutched and pulled his twin p89z, military-issued pistols, and started waving them over his head!

"Hold up Bru!" Said the nervous customer thinking he was about to get jacked.

"Oh, my bad, you straight!" Said Brainhead, motioning with the pistols toward the pack. "Nigga I be rappin and trappin. Watch dis freestyle!" Said Brainhead as he began rapping to the Rick Ross song. "This nigga wild!" I was saying to myself as I stepped out of my white drop head phantom coupe Rolls Royce. Brainhead, my lil potna /brotha/ goon was the flagship artist on my new record label, R.I.C.O entertainment. A young henchman, with some goons under him, surprisingly muscled his way into the rap game just bullshitting around in my studio.

I had got my trucking company logistics off the ground and was running good within 6 months. I'm getting 800 to 1,000 kilos of good nearly raw blow! 10 to 15,000 lbs. of weed straight from Mexico. I had to get a couple of more farms for all this work! I got a farm right outside of Jacksonville, Florida. Another warehouse and about 10 more 18 wheelers to go along with it. So I can run another logistic trucking company in Columbus, Georgia. A farm out in Macon County near Hurtsboro, Alabama. A farm down in Holatee Trail, Florida. Easy to get to when I'm down in Miami at my 10,000 square foot mansion there. My Luis V luggage and duffle bags stayed packed because at any given time I'm on the road making money, and orchestrating plays wherever I'm at!

The life of a hustler! A big-time hustler though! If I'm in Vegas kicking it with my white partner from high school Chauncey. If the supply out there is low and demand is high for some good coke. I'll have one of my 18 wheelers come through and supply the town. Just an example of how I'm getting down! "Nigga you must think it's 1989 or sumthin?!" I asked Brainhead, raising his awareness for real.

"Oh-oh wusup Big Bru!!" Smiled Brainhead, in a "Damn you caught me trippin look!" He was a young gangsta, but he still respected me. "Just checkin on you! I heard you were over here, so I decided to drop through and see what's crackin!" I said.

"Same ole, same ole, Big Bru! Getting to the money!" Said Brainhead, "You talked to Marco?" Asked Brainhead. Referring to the assistant of my record label. "Yeah... Everything is set up for tomorrow! The video shoot and all!"

"Who gone shoot it? Lil X? I know they got us a budget to handle that." Said Brainhead. My record label had sealed a deal with Atlantic once they caught wind of Brainhead's single and the numbers they were doing on the sound scan.

"Yeah... He going to do it. It's going to be shot right here in the A! We hittin da gutter spots and a couple of strip clubs! Nigga y'all... get y'all shit together. It's goin down!" I said hyping these young niggaz on up.

"Oh-oh, I got to have da Lac in my video! Wit dat tool in my hand!" Said Brainhead.

"Pull da donks out nigga!" Said one of Brainhead's goons. We discussed a lil more business before I left. These young niggaz are handling their business in these streets! With the exotic weed and oh... The extortion games!!

(2 Months Earlier)

Brainhead and his crew are already the types of niggaz who were Jack Boys. When they were younger down for the beef, they will act an ass with that gunplay. So, it was nothing to check some niggaz when they got in their lanes or my lane with the bullshit! I tried not to operate like that! You know putting down the muscle game with the violent drama and all but, sometimes there comes a time when niggaz need chastising! Like my nigga Blackjack would say and I am a nigga from the '80s and '90s when the word loyalty meant something! A way of life and niggaz was crewed up and click tight! Street organized crime type of shit. Only now I'm taking things to the corporate level and gangsta! Mobbed up! Shit kind of got crazy when these lil niggaz over on the south side had crossed Brainhead. One or 2 of his lil partners over there was throwing the loud weed on by the pound!

So, some of Brainhead's lil partners and ex-plug, a nigga named Faygo got on some more shit with them. Like saying they can't hustle their product on that side of town period! That's when the shit started!

At first, Brainhead was letting the shit slide until one night he was over there supplying and serving his partners and the opposition sent some flunkies over to their spot trying to intercept the drop-off. I heard the plot through this fine assed stripper named Candy who danced at the Magic City. I had banged the pussy one night, and she told me through some pillow talk and a blunt of cush that the nigga Faygo was on some hating shit. That he was going to send some young niggaz over to see Brainhead and his lil partners the next time he hears or sees them over that way. I laced my lil brother Brainhead up to the plot.

So, on that same night, they came! When they came through little did, they know that Brainhead had his lil goons outside hiding in the dark. So, when they got ready to kick the door, they were met from behind by 4 niggaz strapped with some choppers equipped with infra-red beams.

"Whoa! What y'all niggaz bout to do?!" Said Dingo. As he led the way by hitting one of the would-be robbers in the head with the stock of the A.K.

"Augh!!" Hollered the masked-up thug. It was four of them also, so each one of Brainhead's ambush squad had a man drawn down on. The door opened and the robbers were ushered in. One tried to buck and make a break back out the door. "FWOP!!" Thundered the Glock 40 as the bullet penetrated the back of the would-be runner's skull exploding the front of his forehead and slamming him into the door.

"Whoa!! Hold up Dawg!" Screamed one of the robbers as Brainhead beat on his head with the butt of the smoking pistol. "Who sent yo Bitch ass!" Said Brainhead as he stomped the robber.

"Aaawww! Augh... Augh! Holdup man! Faygo! Faygo sent us man! Please don't kill me, man!" Screamed the robber.

"Dat nigga set us up! Dat nigga put us on a dummy lick!" Said another one of the face-down robbers.

"Turn over nigga!" Said Dingo as he kicked the second robber in his ribs forcing him to lay face up.

"Take off dat mask!" Commanded Brainhead.

Dingo snatched the mask off. "Uhh- huh!!" Said Brainhead as he looks into the eyes of one of his cousin's lil partners. "Damn my nigga, I ain't know yo wit da fuck shit!" Brainhead had been looking out for this nigga on the strength of his cousin.

"Man, I didn't know what was goin on. Who they was talkin bout getting and..." FWOP!!" Augh!" Screamed the robber in agony after Brainhead shot him in his knee cap.

"Shut the fuck up nigga!" Said Brainhead. "I tell you what... where yo phone nigga?!" Brainhead was going through the robber's pockets and grabbed his phone. "Here" Said Brainhead as he was handing the phone to the robber. "Call that nigga Faygo!"

Dude was in so much pain trying to hold his knee, he couldn't focus much on making the call.

"Give me da mothafucka!" Said Brainhead getting impatient as he went to the contacts and found Faygo's number.

"Yo! Wusup?! Y'all handle dat?" Said Faygo as he answered the phone.

"Yea-Yea-Yea, my nigga, dey handled DAT aight!!" Said Brainhead in his signature rapid flow. The phone went deathly quiet for a couple of seconds. "Aye, nigga you still there?" Asked Brainhead.

"Hey Bru who dis?!" Asked Faygo.

"You need to find you some more goons, Bru! These niggas sweet and soft as fuck! Look at these niggaz!" Said Brainhead as he took a picture of the would-be robbers lying on the floor. One of them facedown at the door dead, shot in the back of the head. One grippin a bloody knee, and the other one on his back with an assault rifle pressed against his jaw. "You still there nigga?!" asked Brainhead.

"Maan who the fuck this is?!" Hollered Faygo on the other end of the phone, obviously mad and scared!

"Nigga calm yo bitch ass down before I go see yo mama!" Said Brainhead.

"My ma..." "Yeah yo mama! Bitch ass nigga!" Interrupted Brainhead. "Now check this out... Potna! This what it is for now on since you want to play gangsta and send some lames to do a gangsta's job. When I see a nigga holding any work or any nigga affiliated wit yo Busta ass they gon have to turn something in!"

"Turn something in?!" Questioned Faygo.

"Yeah turn something in... lame!" Said Brainhead.

"Nigga, you know who you fucking wit?!" Screamed Faygo and with that Brainhead shot, the robber who was clutching his knee in the head two times and Dingo shot the other one in the face with the assault rifle.

"Nigga, that's what I think about yo duck ass!" Then sent him a pic of his slain partners. "Nigga matter of fact, when I see you uma put that F and N on you if you don't pay me my shit!!" And with that Brainhead hung up the phone and walked out of the spot.

Faygo was furious as he paced the floor after throwing his phone and busting it against the wall. It wasn't a good 24 hrs. After that, Brainhead's crew and affiliates had started their extortion campaign!

"Man wusup Bra?!" Said the guy from Mobile, Alabama who was getting caught in the crossfire. He was visiting and copping pounds from one of Faygo's Lieutenants. " "Dis."

Said Lansky casually as he shot him in his thigh with the silenced .45 Magnum. "Augh! What the fuck!!" Screamed the Mobile Trafficker.

"Sorry Bra!! You got caught up in the crossfire." Said Brainhead as he grabbed the duffle bag which sat on the couch beside him and Faygo's lieutenant. They had been scoping his lieutenant as soon as they left the previous robbery gone bad scene.

"Call Faygo nigga!" Said Brainhead as he aimed the F and N assault pistol at Faygo's lieutenant and with no hesitation he speed-dialed him.

"Wusup shawty?" asked Faygo on the other end.

"Ay Bru... dey got me." Said the lieutenant.

"What?!" Asked Faygo sounding startled.

By then Brainhead was snatching the phone "Hey old bitch ass nigga! You know who this is?!" Said Brainhead. "This strike two! Um coming at you Bwoy!! Um on yo ass nigga! You better tell the rest of yo niggaz be ready to turn something in! This shit like the state property movie! Get down or lay down!"

Brainhead hung the phone up and shot Faygo's partner in the head and Lansky shot the Mobile, Alabama trafficker in the head. They grabbed the duffle bag of money, the duffle bag with the pounds of loud, a couple of bricks of cocaine, and left.

The next couple of days the city was in a buzz about what was going on in the streets with these young niggaz off the West Side, who are extorting Faygo and whoever else wants to buck and not turn something in! The word was that these dudes hustle and one of them was an up-and-coming rapper.

"I know who they are," I said to my old school cousin out of Adamsville.

"You do?" He asked with curiosity in his eyes.

"One of my lil potnaz chastising Faygo for trying to put down on him hating. So, he's putting back down on him."

"Well, you need to stop him cuz. They're making shit hot and one of my potnaz out of New York named Big Lo be fuckin wit Faygo wit the coke." Said my Cuzzin Alvin.

My cousin had stopped by my studio record label headquarters to talk which was a morning ritual. That was when we smoked joints of Cali, discussed family and business. I gave it a lil thought while cuz looked at me expectantly.

"What you going to do cuz?" Asked Alvin. That's when I picked up my iPhone and texted Brainhead. (Come to the studio when you get a chance!) "He'll be over to holla at me cuz," I said, as I sat my phone back down.

"Good... talk some sense into the youngsta! You... we don't need no big ass drug war going on in the city! That's gonna draw too many Feds, ATF... all types of alphabet boyz! You out of all folks should know when dope boys war. It brings Bussin dem big ole guns shootin and killin folks!" Said Alvin, as he was heading out the door. Stopping and looking back as he put on his Versace shades for effect. "Serious cuz and wit dat um gone!"

No doubt cuz was right. Not to mention all of us had felonies and wasn't trying to go back to the pen! Since I've been out, I brought my cousin back up! He was his old self-driving Jags, Lacs, big pretty trucks, and living in exclusive houses! Developing and training those who have been loyal can create a sense of family. That's very important to the well-being of the whole organization.

So, I accept my cousin's hippin and grooming, and I do the same towards the youngins under me.

"Wusup Big Bru?!" Said Brainhead as he swaggered in my office. We bumped fists as he sat across from me at my desk.

"Oh, um just koolin," I said as I lit up a cigarillo of some O.G. Cush. "Dig this... you might need to slow yo role fuckin wit dat nigga Faygo."

"Man, I might kill dat bitch!" Said Brainhead right before he hit the blunt. "Dat nigga didn't have no business trying to get in my business! You feel me?!" "I don't bother none of these niggaz. Ever since I been out I've been chillin! Fuckin hoes and getting me some money!"

"I feel ya lil Bru!" I said. "Don't get me wrong I understand exactly where you're coming from! Um just saying though... we got to think about your rap career! You bout to blow up my nigga! This label gonna be like rap-a-lot, suave house, death-row, no limit, and cash money in the 90's when they were on fire! You see how yo single jumpin nigga?!"

"Yea, yea, yeah, I feel ya bru, but..."

"But hold up... check this lil bru," I said interrupting Brainhead. "These folks da police are hot as hell and trying to figure out what's going on! We don't need no extra heat and we don't want that nigga goin to the police!"

"That nigga wants war!" Said Brainhead. "he told this lil young nigga who be fuckin my cousin Annette! Said he going to put a hit on every nigga who fuck with me!"

With that, I got quiet because that could mean me too! This nigga Faygo trying to make my whole empire fall! With that kind of shit in the air if he's actually for real my record label and everything else will be in jeopardy! They are my investments and income-generating assets... Including my people in the streets and up-and-coming artists. Got to protect that and protect me as well! They know that I'm down with Brainhead! He's not getting a chance to fuck with me!

I started scheming on how to end this shit and quickly. "My nigga," I said as I stood and put on my coat. "Y'all stand down and lay low for a minute. "

"Lay low?" Said Brainhead as he also stood. "Lay low for what?!" "Man, Antonio, fuck that nigga! We just gon lay down?! Sheeit! Man, I say we..."

"Be cool my nigga!" I said interrupting Brainhead, just before walking out of the office. "I got dis!" I said reassuring my lil partner with a grin on my face.

He hesitated a lil before saying "Aight my nigga... If you say so! But only for a minute" and with that, we exited the building both clutching our hammers on the low as we headed to our cars.

Later that night, I was periodically riding by Magic City and cold trailing Faygo. I had already got the low down on this dude from the stripper broad Candy. The same one who hipped me to Faygo's plot on Brainhead. She even told me how often he frequented the clubs. She was one of them lil bad hoez from the N.O. wit that killa pussy! The ones like Master P used to talk about. The kind that'll set you up and get you killed! Since I was old school, I didn't trust her ass cause if she'll do it to one nigga, she'll do it to you! My philosophy! So, I didn't get her to clock the nigga moves inside of the club. I had one of my sye-pie-say Haitian niggaz from North Miami texting me from the inside. Also, my Zoe's partner lil cousin who just moved to the A from Opa-Locka North Miami was stripping so she was on the nigga Faygo heavy!!

Rae- Sremurd's song featuring Nick Minaj and Young Thug. "Throw some more" was on and my lil Haitian partner's cousin was giving the nigga Faygo a hell of a lap dance. "Damn Shawty, you got me bout to nut in my pants!" Said Faygo.

"Oh, yea?!" Said the fine Haitian stripper. "Just think what me can do in de bed!" Then, she suddenly spun from the position in his lap to a reverse cowgirl position. "You want to hit it like this?" She asked as she placed her hands on his knees and started grinding hard and slow on his bulging dick.

"Ah yeah! Ah, hell yeah!" Said Faygo. "What dat ticket on dat pussy shawty?"

"Nut-ting! You got mi pussy throbbing! I'll give it to you for free!" Said the stripper.

"Well let's go! Now!" Said Faygo. He was horny as hell! He was so caught up that he didn't recognize the lil Haitian broad dropping the molly in the drink.

"Slow down daddy, me have to get permission to leave early."

"Fuck dat!" Said Faygo, "What it's going to cost for you to leave?!" "Who I need to talk to?!"

"Wait... let me go and holla at de' manager!" Said the stripper. She grind on Faygo a couple of deep hard times and quickly got up and sashayed off in the direction of the manager's office.

Leaving Faygo's dick so hard that he almost had the blue

balls. "Shit!" Said Faygo as he sat there grabbing his dick on the verge of masturbating, 3 minutes later she came back and leaned into his ear and said, "He'll let me leave for two hunnid dollars!" Faygo quickly gave her two hundred dollars bills and she quickly walked off.

Actually, the manager told her for a hundred dollars she can leave, but what the hell, she'll make an extra $100 dollars to go along with the $1,000 dollars she was going to make just to trick this nigga off somewhere for her cousins. She didn't know I was involved. When she came back to Faygo he was sweating like hell and grabbing his dick at the sight of her.

"Daddy, what kind of car are you in?" Asked the stripper.

"A light blue corvette." Said Faygo. "Go ahead and pull around the side exit door and I'll meet you there." "Said the stripper". Without questions, Faygo immediately headed for the door. He came with 5 of his partners/goons but since he was thinking with the head in his pants. He forgot all about the goons and most importantly the drama he's in and who and what kind of dudes he's really into it with... killaz!!

(Here he comes!) Texted my partner from inside of the club. I had just pulled in the parking lot in a black Taurus a minute before the text. I texted back (Bet!) As I was backing into a parking spot Faygo came out of the club walking kind of fast over to his Vette while grabbing his dick! A minute later, out comes the stripper fully clothed sashaying over to Faygo's Vette as he pulls up to get her. As they pulled off, I was right behind them careful not to trail them too close.

I sent her a text for her to get him to pull over at the next gas station. Tell him she had to pee real bad. She didn't know who I was, so I told her I was with her cousin. That's all it took.

"Baby hurry up! I'm bout to bust off!" Said Faygo with his exposed dick in his hand. The stripper had been giving him some head as they rode.

"Okay baby, it won't take me long!" Said the stripper as she ran to the bathroom. I pulled around the gas station to dodge any possible cameras and got out with my ski mask and silencer on my 9mm. I quickly made it around to Faygo's Vette from the front. Surprising the shit out of him because he was so horny he was sitting in the car masturbating and looking towards the bathroom.

"Shit!!" Said Faygo, as he quickly looked up at me. Eyes bucking open like one of the black actors in those movies portrayed as one of them frightened Jigaboo-negroes! SPIFFT SPIFFT SPIFFT Sounded the .9 mm as I let off 3 quick shots into Faygo's face. I quickly picked up the shell casings and then I ran around to the driver's side of the car to finish him off. SPIFFT SPIFFT SPIFFT Spitted the strap as I let off 3 more shots in his already splattered head. Just as I was letting off the last shot that's when the Haitian stripper was exiting the bathroom "Aaiia!" Screamed the stripper as soon as she stepped out of the bathroom. At that very moment I let off 4 quick shots above her head putting holes in the door she was just exiting causing her to dive back into the bathroom. I ran to the back of the store, jumped in the Taurus, and smoothly pulled off.

Chapter 10

(VIDEO SHOOT & BEYOND)

"Get my money up quick nigga, real shit! Is all I know!" Rapped Brainhead as he ended his verse before his hook started. "All I know is dat real shit, dat real nigga shit!" Brainhead was lip-synching his verses at the video shoot right along with the song like he was a pro!

Ever since this new single been out it's been a street banger earning my independent label a distribution deal. Jeezy, Gotti, and Money Bagg Yo were on the remix and that's what we decided the video would be. With Faygo out of the equation, we didn't have any current known static/ beef to hinder the takeoff of R.I.C.O Entertainment. If I hadn't nipped that problem in the bud. He would've drawn my main flagship artist into some more hands-on street shit than he's already in. Which could've escalated into him catching a murder case by killing Faygo himself in public or worse... He could've got killed! The news of Faygo's death circulated all around ATL as another unsolved murder!

True enough, the streets knew about which click may be responsible for his murder, but the law didn't have enough evidence to arrest and convict anyone yet! Members of his click went into hiding and his whole organization was dismantled!

Nobody in his crew was willing to step up and try and get some get back... except his plug Big Lo, who in turn is one of my cousin Alvin's old plug and friend. Little did I know that Faygo was Big Lo's nephew on the low and that Big Lo had revenge in his heart!

Out in Stone Mountain, Georgia, in a ducked-off mansion. Big Lo from New York was sitting on his leather sofa looking at the TV. He clicked on YouTube, under new releases and that's when he stumbled upon Brainhead's new video.

"Young bitch ass nigga!" Said Big Lo as he looked at the TV through bloodshot eyes. Big Lo had been very upset and disturbed about the death of his nephew Faygo. He tried hard to explain to his sister, Faygo's mother about what happened. However, his explanation was landing on deaf ears. His sister who still lived in New York had sent Faygo to Atlanta 15 years prior. When he was 15 to keep him safe, out of trouble, and to stop him from falling victim to the streets. Big Lo felt as if he failed to keep his promise to his sister because he let his nephew get swallowed up by the streets. Big Lo grabbed the gallon of Hennessy off the table and took a big gulp out of it. He had been on a drinking binge ever since Faygo's death and funeral. He was plotting revenge but, first, he had to get down to the bottom of the drama and who's responsible. Was the hit done by a stranger or was it a result of an ongoing beef he had with the rapper Brainhead? Whose video he's now watching.

"Who pulled the fucking trigger!?" said Big lo as he watched Brainhead's video. He knew that if he got at Brainhead or if anything happened to him that there would be repercussions. He knew Brainhead was down with "Antonio Deangelo", his friend Alvin's cousin. He knew if he touched anybody in the R.I.C.O organization it would mean war! He would rather french kiss a rattlesnake than step on those toes.

"Damn! I got to find a way to get at these niggaz!" said Big Lo as he watched the music video. He was staring intently at the short, light-skinned, and stocky fellow who had his arm around the rapper Brainhead's neck. He was waving a spread of money side to side. smiling with some fly-ass Cartier glasses on.

"Yeah nigga...smile now...cry later!" said Big lo as he picked up his phone and speed-dialed New York.

Chapter 11

It had been a very prosperous 3 yrs. of freedom. It seemed like all the plans I had in my head as I was visualizing and fantasizing while I was in the pen were coming to pass! Crystalizing right before my eyes. I was head of a self-made corporation/entity which owned businesses and I was a black entrepreneur! Independent, black-owned business that was bout it, bout it like Master P back in the days. I was the owner, CEO, and general manager of Deangelo Enterprises. The legal side was on some Jerry Jones Shit! Under the R.I.C.O enterprise umbrella were a couple of businesses I had running so far such as R.I.C.O Entertainment, my record label, my trucking & Logistics company, Deangelo Transportation & warehousing, and Deangelo Real estate investing. I was into buying and flipping houses, Land development, and building subdivisions.

My partners Chee-Chee and Chris were into computer networking, fiber optics installation, and computer programming. They run that so I opened a sports agency managing athletes and a sports bar. This was just the beginning. I had taken an 8-week course from a sports management school. After finishing I interned at a sports agency just to learn the business for about 9 months.

Instead of continuing to work for the agency, I opened my own with 2 more upcoming agents that were fresh out of college. Shit was definitely popping now so I opened a strip club. All my legal businesses are doing big numbers or about to do big numbers! Brainhead was on his second album already after the first one went triple platinum. A rap group plus an R&B thug nigga or should I say a thug nigga that can sing and write some R&B hits! Both had hot singles out and the rap group was called ATL Cartel Life. 3 hard young niggaz. One was from the Bluff, 4th ward, and Edgewood. Their singles are doing big numbers and I'm a legal multimillionaire now! I was an 8 figure nigga not a regular nigga or just a street nigga! An ex-con who started from the bottom with nothing but balls and my word! Sitting in the office of my new sports bar overseeing my accountants and counting the collection of my slick pick tickets. It was football season so gambling on games in some form or fashion was hot! College games and the NFL was poppin!

"200k so far!" said Jamey as he took off his glasses and lit a cigarette. "Still have those 20 piles to count!"

"That's what's up!" I said as I lit a mini cigarillo blunt of some rapper weed.

"Things are going smooth so far." said Jamey as he looked over his books on a laptop."

"You mean we've been getting by or getting away?"

"Getting away?" asked Jamey as if he was confused.

Yea getting away! That's what we used to say in the joint about the ticket man when too many people have not hit him.

Most of the time no one! I was giving Jamey a little prison lingo. "Oh...I understand where you're coming from Antonio!" said Jamey as he quickly caught on. After taking our smoke break we quickly got back to counting the take. We had collected all of the tickets and were checking to see if anybody hit or were there any round-robin payments. For example, if a person played a five pick-ticket and if four of his teams covered the point spread and he played a $10 ticket or better. We gave them a refund. Good business is our motto in this organization. Niggaz already have enemies for no reason at all. But hate caused by you doing yo thang. Would be the only fuel to the fire to ignite any ill feelings they have towards you and that comes from within. I had bankers there also from my numbers racket. Yeah, on some old-school shit running numbers and a couple of number spots! We just modernized it and we broke it down like this. The policy runner/numbers runner was the lowest level in the numbers racket, and they took calls, texts and dashed around from apartments to houses taking bets. A collector in a particular area got two broads and 1 dude.

Next, the pickup man brought the "work/betting" slips from various collectors to a "controller". I had 3 collectors. 2 black dudes and 1 white girl. One controller that was my partner from the valley named Jaheim. I met him in the penal system, and he moved to Atlanta once he got out. He was part of the nation of Islam for a while but, he kind of slid back into the street life. Nothing too heavy though just a little weed and syrup. That purple drank. He had his own Barbershop /Beauty salon in a 2-story building on the east boulevard. The perfect cover-up for a controller because not only did he have a nice flow of traffic at the shop but upstairs he had a bakery. His main office was upstairs in the back of the bakery.

So, the few collectors that reported to him mixed right in with the normal traffic. Jaheim and two other controllers passed it on to a banker the "money man!" The spiral continues upwards to me! The Boss! Playing the numbers is basically a poor man's game, but it is still big business based on the lottery. Like in the '60s, '70s, and '80s! Hundreds of millions of dollars are milked annually out of ghetto areas by the underworld. Last but not least, "Drops". Slang in the numbers game for a collections place for betting slips and money. I switched drop-spots periodically and usually at the last minute without warning! Ducking all the setups! The robbery set up, the police set up any setups! Because of the type of money that be at these spots. I have to stay on my pz and qz! The type of money niggaz will kill for! So, when I pick a spot a couple of shooters are already there in the shadows! Of course, I am strapped! The odds I was playing on some of the number slips was 600 to 1 so a lot of people played and that meant a lot of money was in the office of this sports bar with us now!

"Damn! that's 1.5 mill." I said after re-running money through two money machines for the second time. This was all gambling money! Some of my workers who are involved in the gambling part of my organization got paid day to day and nightly. Some we just paid once a week. After I broke off and paid all my people me and a couple of my shooters made it out the sports bar and to the vehicles. At times like this, a nigga has to move like the president! I got two shooters outside the door and two more sitting in the parking lot in a big black suburban. 2 more outside the back door and 2 passing by the bar in a big G.M.C. Sierra Denali. Everybody got Ak-47s long and short rifles. Me...I got that F and N pistol-rifle! Protection and death around my money! Blood money! Once I made it to the drophead Rolls-Royce, I jumped in and pulled off behind the G.M.C. Sierra was already riding up and down the street followed by the suburban. By me being in the real estate business now. I own property everywhere so nobody in this entourage/ caravan knew where we're heading but me. I grabbed one of my phones and called the driver of the Sierra which happens to be one of my cousins from the deck.

"I'm bout to get in the next lane and pass you so stay behind me until further notice."

"Bet!" answered my cousin as I rode about 5 minutes until I reached the 3rd signal light. I called my cousin and the other shooters who were in the suburban following and told them to stand down. "

Yo I'm good, I'll get at yall later on."

"Okay my nigga!" said my cousin Mario. They kept going as I turned right and drove another couple of minutes before reaching a gated community deep in Buckhead. To my stash house! Well, one of them. I didn't really have to worry about shit happening out there. A lot of rich professional people lived on this end. My cousin from Dec, Mario was the head of my security detail so I didn't have to worry about any of them trying to double back. At least not at the moment. Little did they know I had somebody on their trail! My phone rang as I pulled up to my crib.

"Wusup?" I said as I answered the phone.

"Erythang clear?" said my tail.

"Bru, let me ask you something," said K.J. who happened to be a childhood friend. I pay very good just to be a tail. "Bru, let me ask you something," said K.J. who happened to be the tail.

"Wusup?!" I said

"Do you have anybody following me?! laughed K.J. because you are cautious and noid as hell!"

"You can never be too careful my friend," I said jokingly. Okay, fuck with me later on! said K.J.

"Bet, I got you later on today. I got to get a lil sleep!"

"Aight..aye..nigga you got a hoe over there? You need to take the time out to get you some pussy nigga!" laughed K.J.

"You stay on the move all day and night nigga chasin that money!" I laughed it off with my partner.

"Later nigga!" I said, before hanging up. But he did have a point! I stay on the move handling business and I really did need to slow down and spend more time with my main squeeze! Matter of fact that's what it's going to be for the next couple of days. Bitches!

Chapter 12

RETRIBUTION

"Revenge is just another word for payback." You niggaz knew I wouldn't play that and I'd send you bitches to the morgue with 2 shots 2 da head and no remorse! Why you think niggaz call me the boss because I be dressed up in designer suits? Or the fact that these niggaz know I'm the truth!" Jonathan was in a daze as he listened to a song from scarface's balls and my word CD. In a daze thinking about the new task as he would call it. The task of taking me and my organization down to our deaths! Jonathan flew from Texas by one of Big Lo's people out of New York. These niggaz are still hot bout Faygo's death!

"Yo wusup sunnyside!" Said Big Lo's partner from New York referring to Jonathan under his code name.

"Already, wusup!" Said Johnathan as he raised up from his seat.

"This my man I was telling you bout... who hired you for your new task... Big Stew." Said New York referring to Big Lo under code.

As the two men shook hands Big Lo discretely and quickly sized the youngsta up. Jonathan didn't look like a killer to Big Lo.

"Nigga look like a pretty boy!" Said, Big Lo. "Nuttin close to a killer!" Laughed Big Lo as he looked the Drake look-alike up and down.

"Yea... you right! I am a pretty boy, wit killa bitches!" Drawled Jonathan in his Texas accent as he showed Big Lo the video of his goon with a big pistol equipped with a silencer up against his temple outside of Jonathan's hotel room. The big pistol was being held by a little sexy female who resembled the rapper, DJ Loaf.

"Wusup Boo? You want dis nigga erased!" Purred the lil sexy killer.

"Naw, March that nigga up in here!" Said Johnathan, speaking into his watch phone.

"What about the nigga in the car?" Said the female as she marched Big Lo's goon into the room. She was referring to Big Lo's driver who was outside in a black Navigator held at gunpoint by the girl's twin sister. Killer twins from the 3rd ward in Houston, Texas.

"Tell her to stay there with him for a minute!" Said Johnathan. The girl relayed the message to her twin.

"Already! Um up in the truck with him anyway!" Said, Twin.

"Okay... ya'll ready to get down to bizness?!" Said Johnathan who was looking Big Lo in the eyes as he smiled. Big Lo looked at Johnathan and slowly looked at the sexy killer with his goon at a standstill and then at his New York homeboy. Shook his head up and down. Looked back at Johnathan with an approving smile and said "Let's do business! But first, call off your... um... shootaz." Said Johnathan finishing Big Lo's sentence for him. "Yeah!... shootaz!" Repeated Big Lo.

Meanwhile, as Big Lo and his hit team were in a hotel room plotting on me and my team. I was in the Virgin Islands with a girl who was my main squeeze. Since I've been out, I call her my main squeeze because I give her the most attention and have some feelings for her. Out of all the bitches I fuck with she's the one! Oh... and I can trust her to a certain degree. Her name is Tanya, and she was a female friend from my past before I fell and went to prison. Tanya and I used to flirt and talk with each other on occasion but nothing serious. True enough I wanted to fuck her and make her my girl and all that! Because I love some redbones and Tanya stood about 5'6", 145 lbs. give or take. China doll face with the almost juicy lips to match! A little thicker than Rhianna. Modest, but jazzy with a little flash, professional, and down to earth. Wifey material! But nevertheless, we remained friends. Besides, she had a man that was a good boy wannabe dope boy on the college campus of Georgia Tech. She was still digging me and my thug-style bad boy persona!

In the middle of my bid Tanya and I started communicating through letters and cards a little, but with her going to college and working and me being locked up with her boyfriend for years doing federal time. Years later at the end of my bid, Tanya and I linked up via Facebook, then cell phone, and finally visits! She rode it out with me till I got free. She had been separated from her ex way after he got out. So, I caught her at the right time, and she was there for me. It was only right for me to give her some of my time! Since I'm out and able to get to her like I want and need to!

One thing led to another and the next thing you know. Me, Tanya, and her daughter were living in a 10,000 sq. ft. mansion out in Lithonia! With foreign cars parked all over the place! Tanya was smart and connected with a lot of professional people. She had a friend who worked in a bank who would give her the heads up on some homes like what's about to go into foreclosure. We would go ahead and buy a couple for the low-low and triple our money on the sale! Kind of like insider trading! Her and my cousin ran my real estate investing company. Shuwanda had experience working with mortgages thru a company out in Dunwoody, Georgia. So, everything was smooth there!

"What's up Boo? You got something on yo mind?" Asked Tanya as she walked up hugging me from behind letting her hands find their way to my dick. "Wusup?! Talk to me Boo." Said Tanya her soft, sexy voice in my ear as she gently squeezed and stroked me through my off-white Linen Polo shorts. I was out on the balcony of our ocean-front condo. We had just got through smoking a mini cigarillo of some exotic ass island cush. So, she was feeling good as hell and drinking Hennessy! Making me think about a scene from the Dej-Loaf video "Me, Hennessy and You!" When she was walking the beach by the ocean and things! Because Tanya had on the exact style-bathing suit and little Robe! Now she got me amped up! Ready to get on some porn-star shit!

"Oh, nuthin Boo. I'm just thinking!" I said in a husky voice because she got me all horny!"

"I thought this supposed to be our vacation. You out here thinking about money, making plays, and scheming!" Said

Tanya as she released my throbbing dick from my shorts and slowly stroked it.

"Well, do you mind if I stroke you up?" Said Tanya in a singing manner imitating the old song from "Changing Faces". And I went right along with-it singing R Kelly's part, "I don't mind!" And she comes back with the other part, "Do you mind if I stroke you down!" "I don't mind." I sang as I turn to face her and taking off my tank top at the same time. Tanya was snatching my shorts and boxers down. She leaned into me and stuck her tongue in my mouth while stroking my dick at the same time!

As I proceeded to meet her kisses, I felt a warm tingling sensation on my shaft and head of my wood! Tanya had done slid some strawberry-flavored motion lotion on me! Her favorite flavor! I started rubbing her head and running my fingers through her hair, both hands! She knew what time it was! She immediately slid her tongue from my mouth and dropped to her knees and grabbed my dick and slowly stroked it as she blew her breath on it to fully activate the sensations of the motion lotion.

"Oooo shit Boo! Don't play wit me!" I said yearning for some head.

"Umm, umm, I got you Boo!" moaned Tanya as she slowly put the head and 2 inches of me in her hot mouth. I had my right hand on her head guiding her right into my slow hunches and grinds! Slow fucking her mouth as if it were a pussy! Shit so good make a nigga wanna sing! Then she's putting those pretty brown eyes on me because she knows like Pimp C said, "I like to look her in her eyes when she sucks it! We're out here freaking on the balcony of our ocean-front condo-like some porno stars! One thing about it though, we own the whole building! Anyway, I didn't want to cum just yet.

I snatched my dick out of her mouth and like clockwork she was snatching her swimsuit off and I was turning her around and bending her over. She was spreading her ass cheeks and I was ramming my dick up in her tight pussy like it was last time I would fuck her!

"Daaam Baby! You mad at me about something!" Said Tanya as she was reaching back placing her right hand on my stomach as if to slow my thrust down. Yet she was throwing that pussy back on me! Truth be told at that moment I was thinking about the times I was locked up and she was too busy to fuck with me like I wanted and needed her to! Or when I've called her and she wouldn't accept my call! Maybe her nigga was around at the time! I don't know and I could've been wrong. Nevertheless, I am a vengeful person and a Scorpio! When I was locked up, I added fuel to my fire list! All the things that were negative in my eyes or happened to me fueled my fire and desire to get free and rich! That shit worked! Laws of Attraction! By now I had zoned out and got a handful of her hair. I started pulling it and fucking her hard like she's a thot or something!

"Oh-Da-Daamn Bae! You mad at me?" Moaned Tanya referring to how I was fucking her.

"Nawl Boo!" I said as I reached around and put my middle finger on her clit! Truth was I was thinking about a time or two when she wouldn't accept my call! So yeah... I'm vengeful to a fault at times.

"Uumnh, umnnh, ooo, oo shit! Daamn! Sss!' moaned

Tanya as she started to drip cum down my fingers invoking me to blast off status!

"Sssssss, shit!" I hollered as I emptied my load into Tanya. Damn near collapsing! Me and Tanya made our way back into the condo and took our hot sex to the bedroom. While I was in the Caribbean Islands making love to my girl doing the snake off in that pussy. Some snakes back in the United States were plotting to make me a pussy!!

-

Chapter 13

GAME TIME

My supposed getaway to the Virgin Islands for a couple of days turned into a month's vacation! True enough I had said that I won't be on no business type of shit while we are down there but, some things came up. First of all, me and Tanya's real estate company owned the oceanfront condos we've been vacationing in. Leasing them out as timeshare properties and we have 100 condos in this building. We lease them for $20,000 a year through my attorney in Birmingham, Alabama Janice Riddlesburg the ex-wife of my former attorney. The one I seduced & knocked off to help me get out of prison. I had her set me up an offshore corporation named Aniyavest in GA and all of it is under my R.I.C.O organization. It served as one of the conduits for channeling drug money. Mostly my weed money went into this apartment complex in the Virgin Islands with a full-fledged spa/resort. Money laundering! Money was laundered by many off-the-books and under-the-table transactions with the sub-contractors involved in the construction of the apartment complex. Now, I was in the midst of investing in other businesses down there like another resort! Then I caught a deal on a yacht that was a 100-footer. I called my attorney Janice Riddlesburg to make it happen.

"Okay, Antonio I'll get right to it but, let me ask you this..."

"Yea Janice wusup?" I asked with my alarm going off in my head.

"When are you going to give me the dick?!"

"Ha, ha! soon baby!"

"Ha hell." Said Janice. "Just as soon as you get back to the states!"

"Okay, okay, I got ya Janice."

"I'm serious Antonio!" Said Janice and hung up.

I haven't been fucking her much since I've been out. Matter of fact only a couple of times. As soon as I get back, I'm off to Birmingham to freak her a whole weekend! She looks like Meg Ryan with those striking light-steel blueish eyes and wavy blond hair almost shoulder length. Petite build with a nice lil round booty and some little hips which poke out. I enjoyed fucking with her, but I've been so busy which made it hard for me to just spend time with her. Unless I'm coming with a couple of duffle bags of money from a lot of weed transactions which I need her to help me clean up.

By now the game escalated on all levels for me! Big business on the illegal side! Fucking with my Amigos I'm distributing serious weight in weed, cocaine, and heroin! So much that I had to set up more businesses to funnel, clean money, and sho-nuff setup & expand a loose and informal Amoeba-like infrastructure that controls my secret criminal network. Somewhat tightening up and organizing my street business to the point of watching it micromanaging things!

At this point, one shop I'm supervising is a large network that distributed multi-ton quantities of good marijuana. By now my numbers with my plug Anita are so low that any ticket I put on my bales is profit! I had 2 people who worked directly under me who in turn had six people working for them selling and fronting their bales. These buyers in turn had their own employees in the network. I ran a highly structured and well-organized distribution network.

I had my cousin Bam-Bam in Jacksonville, Florida collecting payments from my weed. Held most of it till I came and laundered some of it through her modeling agency or other small ventures like beauty salons and nail shops. I take the bulk of that money to my attorney in Birmingham to clean through my offshore corporation Aniyavest, GA. The marijuana was usually distributed in quantities ranging from 28,000 lbs. to 32,000 lbs. There was a whole network of drivers. Deliveries and pickups could only be made between 8:00 am and 5:00 pm Monday – Saturday. Employees in the operation had fixed weekly salaries. It wasn't long before my weed distribution network expanded outside of Florida, Georgia, Alabama and Mississippi were getting some of my weed. South and North Carolina and speaking of South Carolina ole girl Kadia was still speaking on the disappearances of her cousin Brad and his cousin. I wanted to tell her the catfishes done ate them up by now in the Chattahoochee River!

Instead, I started steering clear of her not knowing that was making her even more suspicious! I had some people in Nashville, Tennessee distributing my weed and whatever else! A lot of work was moved through my trucking logistics company. After tying up all the loose ends down in the islands we flew back to the states to get back to business.

I had restructured and reorganized my cocaine and heroin distribution network in the same style as my weed distribution network. That way I can micro-manage a little better. Sitting up in my office of Deangelo Enterprise downtown Atlanta, catching up on my street business as well as my legal business. I'm looking over my record label roster checking sales, pending releases, and new artists who my A&R people were looking at.

"Who is this Drake-looking nigga?!" I asked no one in particular as I looked at my computer screen. He had been recording with my people while I was gone. I clicked on the tab to see how the Drake look alike sounded.

"Damn! This nigga rockin." I said, as I grabbed one of my phones and called my assistant Marco who was my COO (Chief Operation Officer) at Rico Entertainment. Which is in another location that I own. I'm now at the head office of Deangelo Enterprise.

"Yo wusup Antonio?!" asked Marco as he answered my call.

"Back to bizness! Aye... who dat Drake looking nigga y'all been recording wit?"

"Oh, dats Johnathan from Texas! Dat nigga nice ain't he?!" Said Marco getting all hyped up.

"Yea, dat nigga rockin! So where did y'all find him at?"

"Shit, Antonio dat nigga just popped up out of nowhere! Serious! We koolin at the strip club one night while you were vacationing and "...Which club?" I interrupted.

"Yo club potna!" Said Marco.

"Oh, okay! Go head my nigga, my bad!"

"Yeah... I don't know how the nigga knew who I was, but he came in the V.I.P. with 2 bad twin broads like yo... I got something you would be interested in. And handed me a CD and um like Bru can this wait? And he was like nawl! Matter of fact let me see it. So, he took the CD to the DJ booth and got the DJ to play a song or two off his demo and that shit had the club rockin! He came back to the V.I.P. and gave me a business card. Smooth yet kind of arrogant with them bad bitches and he was about to leave but, I stopped him in is his tracks and told him to come to the studio the next day. And just like dat da nigga showed up and showed out!"

"Just like dat huh?!" I asked.

"Just like dat Antonio! I knew you would like him! What you thinking?! You think we ought to sign him?" Asked Marco.

Me being the type of nigga I am which was suspicious almost to a fault. I was to meet Johnathan face to face! Look the nigga in his eyes and see what type of vibe I pick up! I try not to bring my animal instinct into the legal business world. At least not at such a high magnitude, but the music industry is a jungle in its own way.

So, fuck it my street antenna overrules my judgment and decision-making! Making whoever feels the vibe of thoroughness, realness, and loyalty as a way of life. So, if they some fake-snake suspect mufuckas time going to tell on ya. No matter how much talent they got or how much money they'll be bringing or potentially bringing to the label. If they need to be watched then that's what it will be. If they need to be dealt with... that's what it will be.

"Set up a meeting wit me and this cat at the studio!" I said to Marco.

"That's wusup! It's on you, Antonio! When are you going to be free?"

"Shit... set up a meeting for 12 tomorrow afternoon."

"Got ya Bru!" Said Marco as he hung up.

Sitting in my office at the studio while smoking some exotic with Marco and Brainhead. I noticed the rapper, Johnathan, on the security screen. As he approached the entrance I said, "here the nigga comes now." as I passed the blunt.

The Drake look alike is being put through the metal detector by my security.

"Damn! Y'all got security on point around here! I feel safe already!" Said Johnathan being sarcastic as he's being shown in.

"Hey, wusup Johnathan." Said Marco as he got up and shook hands with him.

"Already, wut it do?!" Said Johnathan.

"Johnathan, this Antonio the CEO /Owner of RICO Entertainment. Antonio this is Johnathan the one I was telling you about from Texas!" Said Marco making the introductions.

"Wut it is?!" I said as I came from around my desk to shake his hand. The whole time I'm making eye contact, weighing the dude up, and checking his temperature at the same time! Trying to see what kind of vibe I'm getting off the dude. I'm like that by habit. Growing up in the hood running the streets and going to prison for a long bid. Will have a nigga on point and game-tight! That's if you're smart!

"Already! Man, I heard a lot about you!" Said Johnathan.

"Oh yeah?" I said because my red flags were up! What had this dude heard about me besides my being CEO and owner of R.I.C.O entertainment? Okay... I might be paranoid, so I'll let it go... for now.

"Yea maine! Heard nothing but good things." Said Johnathan. "This nigga can stand some watching," I said to myself.

"That's wusup!" I said pushing the conversation on. "Have a seat Johnathan and let's talk business. First of all, you don't have an agent or manager?"

"Do I need one?" Said Johnathan.

"Well... not necessarily, just proper business practices.

"Well, I'll take that into consideration later, but right now I'm my own manager." Said Johnathan.

"Okay... ain't nothing wrong with that as long as you know the business side of the game. I like to do square bizness with no bullshit ya feel me?!"

"Already! What... y'all plan on signing me?" Johnathan said with a sly smirk on his face.

Marco and I exchanged a look. I looked at Brainhead as well. He had a smirk on his face. I slowly said... "Yeah! We going to sign you!"

"Already!" Said Johnathan as we shook hands.

"Welcome to RICO Records... Fam!"

Chapter 14

It had been a couple of years since Carlos Desendez had lost his son at the hands of some African American hitman. He can still hear the shots, screams, and cries of his son as he was being shot at close range while standing over a hole that he fell in. It was his grave in a desert. He could tell from the background. Well, the little background he had seen. It was so dark on the video which was sent by the killer from his son's phone to his and Mexico was full of desert land.

Carlos Desendez had been in the witness protection program for the last 8 years. His handlers, the Feds kept close tabs on him through a series of agents. Three or four of them, but he only reported to one while the other 2 or 3 played the shadows and followed him while he did his daily routine. Carlos knew this though since he was a very cunning person. Naturally, he'd picked up on their so-called surveillance. Carlos was raised in the trenches of Mexico in the rural area of Soliceno and he frequented the city of Matamoros as a child. That's where he met Garcia Abregado and started his life of crime.

At the young ripe age of 12, Carlos and Garcia had been petty criminals at first. Stealing, burglarizing cars, homes, and targeting tourists by pickpocketing them. They even built up their nerves to commit a few robberies. They both had come from poor families, so it was all about the come-up and the hustle!

Carlos's father was a farmer's helper and he definitely didn't want to follow in his footsteps. Garcia's mother and father both worked in a garment factory for low wages which wasn't enough to feed their 8-children. Garcia is the oldest of the children who took charge to help his parents take care of his other 7-siblings. Especially, his baby sister Conswela! The thought of her being hungry drove Garcia deeper into a life of crime. All the little legal side jobs he would do weren't making enough money.

By the age of 16, Garcia and Carlos had joined a local gang which led to peddling marijuana and kidnapping for ransom. By the age of 18, they both worked for the local cartel. Providing protection to other drug trafficking organizations that needed to move there and work through their turf. Also, they performed hits!

By the '80s their leader and bossman Luis Espanzo was mysteriously murdered in his house in Soto LaMarina, South of Matamoros. This angered Garcia who was now age 20 and very loyal to Luis who mentored Garcia to the dope game and the game of life! Garcia was adamant about finding out who killed his partner Luis.

Luis always told him to follow his gut feelings, instincts, and what they were telling him about a matter. While the rest of Luis's organization acted as if they were bewildered about what was going on Garcia wasn't!

Oscar Medrano, Luis's 3rd in charge was acting real peculiar to Garcia. Luis's right-hand man and 2nd in charge Francisco had come up missing and later found murdered in

Brownsville, Texas which Garcia found out was a stash house! Garcia always suspected Oscar of being a snake. He could always tell that Oscar was a jealous-hearted man and he could also tell he wanted to be "The Man"!

Garcia's gut instinct told him that the housekeeper knew something. He could tell the way she was acting after the body was found. She had an alibi because she was off that day at her daughter's house helping her clean up. But the day before she was at the ranch cleaning up the house. Once Garcia caught up with her, his instincts were right! She knew enough to convince him that his instincts were on point. She didn't tell the policia out of fear of retaliation.

Also, she didn't tell anyone out of the organization because she didn't trust any of them besides Garcia. She told Garcia that she had stumbled upon Luis and Oscar having a heated argument about a guy name Fernando and his protection fee to move a load of cocaine and weed through their turf. She said she heard Oscar saying something about being unfairly cut out of the deal for being the middleman because he is the one who brokered the deal between him and the Columbian drug trafficker named Fernando who was seeking permission from Luis to move his load through Matamoros.

So, Garcia put 2 and 2 together and figured out the play. Somehow Fernando got to Luis himself and made the deal cheaper by cutting out the middleman. So, Oscar killed Luis & robbed him for the dope, which was being stored at the ranch waiting to be transported to Matamoros and then across the border to Brownsville to a stash house. Then he went to Brownsville and killed Francisco or had him killed then took the dope at the stash house.

After the murder, the organization was dismantled except for a few who were loyal to Oscar. Garcia knew that Oscar wouldn't trust him due to his loyalty to Luis. So, he kind of went incognito to make it easier to sneak up on him and murk him!

And that's exactly what he did! Right at the time when Fernando was to bring his load through Matamoros. Garcia and Carlos assembled their own little crew and captured a member of Fernando's crew. Then, they beat information out of him concerning the time, place, how the load would be delivered, and the underhanded deal put together by Fernando and Oscar. The deal was to cut Luis all the way out of the equation. Garcia and his crew were on point when the load landed by murdering everybody who was there including Oscar!

Garcia and Carlos got the load of drugs and went to one of Oscar's stash houses and recovered the remaining stash of Luis's dope which Oscar took from him and started their own organization. Garcia, being the loyalist he was made sure to take care of Luis's family. Garcia got in touch with a few of the old members of Luis's distribution network in the United States and began supplying them with the drugs. Garcia got in contact with Luis's old plug and made deals. From there, he started his own cartel with his childhood friend Carlos Desendez as his right-hand man and his childhood sweetheart Anita as his first lady.

As far as the eye could see everything was cool between Garcia and his right-hand man Carlos. They both were getting rich. They both were feared and ruthless men, but there was a flaw in Carlos. He had always been envious of Garcia on the low. Something bout how people gravitated towards Garcia but would never take notice of Carlos. Not to mention how the ladies gravitated towards Garcia! That was the straw that broke the camel's back! When Garcia got Anita way back in their middle school days. Carlos had a spark of jealousy in his heart and over the years that spark grew into a forest fire! Garcia never really paid Carlos's envy any mind. He thought it was minor jealousy, but all the time Carlos wanted to be Garcia.

So, that's why when it was time to be real and the Federales came. Being real wasn't even in Carlos's vocabulary. He flipped on Garcia without any hesitation and he paid for it in the form of his son's demise. Now, he was out for blood! His little mission was to get back at Garcia and whoever else was involved in his son's death. He knew Garcia had something to do with it because of what was said on the phone. "Don't come back to court!" He knew that Garcia stood a good chance of getting back in court. That's if he didn't show up!

As Carlos was doing his daily routine, he decided this day was the day he would be leaving the witness protection. They had stepped their security surveillance up when Carlos's son was murdered. They had snatched Carlos and his wife and any other family members they could get to.

After a while, the feds allowed them to move around once again and resume their lives under aliases. Carlos had noticed a couple of months ago that when he went to work that he had some rookie federal agent cold trailing him. He would be at this store which was close to the plant where he worked every morning when he got to work. He arrived about 30 minutes before Carlos got off and right before Carlos's lunch break. He cased the side door of the plant and he had a mountain bike hidden in the bushes near the side door. From there he took a side road and pedaled the bike 2 blocks to a nearby neighborhood where he had an old Toyota Camry parked behind an abandoned house.

After about 5 hours on the road, Carlos stopped and got him some rest. As Carlos laid back in a hotel, he was formulating plans in his head like where would he strike first to get the info he needed. "Texas!" Whispered Carlos.

He knew that the feds would be looking for him there, but he didn't care. He knew with the right amount of pressure applied he would find what he needed to know. That's where Garcia's family lived, and he would find out just where!

Chapter 15

"Antonio, I had to have you flown down here and meet with me to tell you the good news in person!" Said Anita.

As we looked out at the ocean, as we sailed out on the Atlantic from Miami Beach on Anita's yacht.

Garcia's lawyer had been working around the clock on Garcia's appeal from his 2255 Federal Habeas Corpus. He was getting good friction with a lot of his issues, but the main one was the government's provision of inducements to its witnesses.

"Garcia is close to getting a new trial! He got a reversal in the Appeals Court and if everything goes right. He stands a strong chance of getting his freedom in the next couple of months!" Said Anita.

"Damn! That's good Anita!" I said as I hugged her. Reading my mind Anita said, "No, I don't think he's showing up in court!" Said Anita, referring to Carlos. "Some of our people informed me that Carlos escaped from witness protection somehow."

"Well, I hope that's a good sign, Anita!"

"Yea... me too!" Said Anita as she looked in my eyes deeply. From my experience dealing with her, I knew what that look meant!

"I need to find him to make sure that he doesn't come to court," I said. Really, halfway asking to see if my instincts were right.

"Yes... He does need to be found!" Said Anita. "Actually, I have somebody on that right now."

The wheels in my head were turning 100 miles per hour! Anita may have had somebody on Carlos's trail, but she also knew that I would put in the work out of loyalty to her and her husband who was my potna!

"Antonio, I know things have picked up tremendously on your end so I wouldn't want to take you out of your schedule... and."

"I'm on it!" I interrupted Anita. She looked at me as if she were weighing my assurance.

"Just wait it out, Antonio. He is a very slippery adversary and a real dangerous one too!"

"I heard!" I said, "I think the element of surprise could down a gorilla!"

"Yes... But we need to find him... besides... the elimination of his son is what drew him out!" Said Anita. "Once we locate him, we quickly will form a plan to erase him!"

"And what about the other witnesses?!"

"They're all doing a bid but are in the process of being dealt with." Said Anita with a gleam in her eyes. "A couple of them will recant their testimony, while the other 3 will probably die mysteriously or in a riot!"

I knew these Mexicans were very powerful and rich. So, to reach into some federal lockups and touch someone wasn't impossible.

"As I said, Antonio... when the time is right, you will be

contacted," Anita said this not knowing that we will see Carlos sooner than we think. The hunted has become the hunter!

Chapter 16

"A record deal?! Man, what type of shit he on?!" Questioned Big Lo, concerning Johnathan's new record deal with R.I.C.O Entertainment.

"That's his strategy yo!" Said Big Lo's people from New York.

"Strategy?!... When this nigga and his lil twin hoes going to dead these niggaz B?! Sounds like he came to Atlanta like the rest of these dream chasers! He supposed to be getting up on these niggaz and whackin 'em!" Said, Big Lo.

"Lo, wit all due respect if it was that easy yo. Seems like you would've been done silencing those cats!" Said Big Lo's New York people.

"Nigga I'm a boss! I've been left that hands-on shit alone!" Said, Big Lo. As he straightened out the imaginary wrinkles in his Armani suit jacket.

"Okay, that's what I mean so let him handle it his way!" Said Lo's NY people.

By now Johnathan had snapped out of his codeine and cush induced nod.

"Look here, Big Lo... Either you gone let me fuck this cat and you hold the tail... nawl matter of fact my twins going to hold the tail. Either you gone do that or I'll just let the cat go and live. Matter of fact, stroke the cat, let it purr for me, and still get rich and famous! So, what's it going to be? Chili sauce or what?" Said Johnathan. In his Morris Day impersonation as he gave one of the twin's high-five.

Big Lo just stared at them for a few seconds before he answered.

"Okay... just make it worth the wait!" Said Big Lo as he left Johnathan's room.

Johnathan was working on his plan. He was working it all the way and it worked itself out! Once he found out he was being hired to knock off an up-and-coming Black-Tycoon. He had to approach it from a different angle. For one, the object was to get away when you made a hit. This dude Antonio was kind of hard just getting up on to shoot without getting caught or seen by somebody. Simply because he kept shooters around plus, he stayed strapped! These targets were gangstafied in an organized way. So, now he was trying to figure out how to get up on him. It was hard to trail him. Johnathan hasn't been to his house, so he didn't know where he stayed. He always got with him at the studio, his office, or one of his strip or jazz clubs. So, he figured he could play up under Antonio through the rap game!

Johnathan's friends and family always encouraged him to rap and take it seriously enough to make a career out of it. Johnathan wasn't really like a lot of other talented young Black men! The streets had allured him with their shine. Johnathan liked the fast money, flashy things, and fast women! He resorted to being a Jack-Boy-Hit man. Jackin and performing hits all through the South, West, even the East coast. That's how Big Lo's people ran across him. He had been up in Jersey putting in work for somebody there and they referred him to possible customers.

So he is now in Atlanta trying to put in work and ran up on a record deal! Everything was smooth with that except that R.I.C.O Entertainment's flagship rapper Brainhead was feeling some type of way. Jonathan didn't know if it's jealousy or what. They did 2 songs together, one for Brainhead's album and one for Johnathan's album.

"Yella ass nigga, it's something bout you! Um doing this song wit you on the strength of Antonio and the label, but straight up bru I don't fuck wit ya!" Said Brainhead, in the studio when they recorded their first song together.

"Already! Likewise nigga! What you mad cause I murdered you on yo own song!?!" Said Johnathan.

Antonio and a couple of the staff members had to get between them. He didn't know if Brainhead was onto him or what. He thought about whackin Brainhead on G.P. general-purpose! He had made himself a promise that when the time was right, he would leave Brainhead wet up and dead! What his focus was on was catching Antonio slipping and do him first. Kill the head and the ass would surely die! Johnathan had already done his homework and found out that Big Lo's nephew had been beefing with Brainhead and his crew from the start. So, he felt it was a must to get at Brainhead. Even with this young fool, it was hard to just catch him slipping so he had to come up with a plan.

With the record deal and all, it was really a blessing and a curse! A blessing because with the money they were paying like the advance with the rest to come with it like points off CD sales, downloads, streams, and show money. it was killing the fee for the contract murders and he could leave the street shit alone, all together! This was something he would have to really think about by weighing the pros and cons.

In all actuality he was a hitman down for making a nigga disappear for the right price... but at the same time, this was what his grandmama used to tell him.

"What the devil meant for bad in yo life, God will take it and guide you through it to make good out of it Jon-Jon!"

Jon-Jon wasn't really all that religious, but he did give that statement some thought. How would it affect his rep in the underworld if he backed out of the hit with no legitimate reason like F.B.I. was onto you! He thought about using these niggaz to get him some fame in the rap world and when the time is right, he would still whack Brainhead and Antonio. Collect the rest of his scratch from these New York niggaz and then use his fame and a small fortune to start his own label.

"That's what it be!" Said Jon-Jon.

Chapter 17

After leaving Anita discussing business. I had caught a flight to Birmingham, Alabama to get with my lawyer Janice Riddlesburg. We had some business to handle like cleaning up this money and putting this dick on her! I was traveling around scouting for my sports agency.

After I leave Birmingham, I have to fly to Louisiana to talk to one of my future clients after the Bayou Classic. He plays with Grambling, a six-foot-three receiver by the name of Dee Banks. He had a bright future and I was trying to help him reach the N.F.L. with some big money for him... and me! He had a fine ass 41-year-old mother who from the first time I met her looked at me like she wanted to eat me alive! She was caramel brown with some Mary J. Blige slanted eyes & lips and an ass that wouldn't quit. Mouth size titties, small athletic waist, nice round hips, and thighs! A body that if a nigga be around her in the house all day his dick will stay hard looking at her strut around in some boy shorts! I'll tell you about the situation later... back to Birmingham, Alabama.

Sitting in Janice's office after hours running money through money machines and preparing bank statements, my phone kept vibing.

"Damn! Who is this?!" I said as I looked at my phone. I

didn't recognize the number, but I still went ahead and answered it. "Hello!"

"Hey Antonio, how are you doing?!"

"Umm... good! Who is this?!"

"I guess it have been a long time since we've talked and you wouldn't know my voice."

My mind was running like crazy for a few seconds and then her voice registered... It was my ex-girlfriend who went sour on me during my bid! I still was smiling because I used to love this lil red-bone high school sweetheart!

"Is this Step?!

"Yeees!" Said Stephanie as she giggled.

"Heeey! How you doing?!" I said with genuine excitement in my voice.

"Um doing good! I seen you in the galleria earlier today, so I called my cousin and she gave me your number."

"Oh... ok." I said slightly stunned.

"Is it cool to talk? I mean you're not busy, are you?" Said Stephanie, sensing that I was in the middle of something.

"Step, actually I am, but I will get back at you later."

"Okay, text me before you call back."

"A'ight," I said as I hung up. My mind was wandering like crazy! Thinking about what made her call me. She couldn't stand the rain like she promised she would, but now that I'm free and rich as fuck I might give her the benefit of the doubt. Let me get back to the business at hand.

"Who was that?" Asked Janice as she walked up on me grabbing my dick and sucking on my neck.

"You goin to start something!" I said, As I reached around and grabbed her ass.

"That what I was hoping!" Whispered Janice as she pulled out my tool as it got bone hard. "You know you owe me." Said Janice as she stroked my dick and squeezed my chest at the same time.

"I pay you good, don't I?" I said as I ran my right hand through her curly hair guiding her to my throbbing dick. I took my shirt off and stepped out of my Armani pants and shoes in one swift motion and rammed my dick deep down Janice's throat, testing her gag reflexes.

"Gagg! MMM, MMM Antonio!" Moaned Janice as she hugged, gagged, and hummed on my dick.

"That's what I'm talking bout Jan!" I said as I slowly fucked her in her mouth while I grabbed two handfuls of her hair and ears.

As I was enjoying Janice's mouth, I heard the door open and it was Jan's thick young secretary, Amanda. A young 21-year-old white girl!

"Oh shit!" I said snatching my dick out of Jan's mouth.

"What's wrong?!" Said Jan.

"Amanda is in here!"

Jan looked up from her position looked at Amanda and smiled. "Close the door Amanda and come on in!"

"What the fuck!" I said as Jan grabbed my shiny dick and commenced sucking as Amanda slowly walked over to where we were at.

"Come on take your clothes off!" Said Jan to Amanda. Amanda smiled at me as she unbuttoned her shirt she threw her arms around my neck and tongue kissed me! I started caressing her young breasts and ass as I unzipped her pants and inserted my middle finger in her wet pussy. "Damn!" I'm thinking to myself because I been wanting to fuck Amanda and I'm thinking I was right about these two! I had been thinking that they had been talking about me, the way they looked at each other when I'm around. Especially, if I fall through there with an under armor shirt on flexing after a workout.

By now Amanda's tight ass slacks were being stepped out of at the same time I was pulling my dick out of Jan's mouth. Amanda bent over and placed her hands on Janice's desk and without hesitation, I was ramming this rod up in her from the back. Janice came up and started tongue kissing Amanda and playing with her clit. About to take Amanda to another level of the game! She's only 21 so it will be a great experience for her.

After handling my business with Janice, I went to my duck off crib out in Greystone and showered. While getting myself together I was checking messages and missed calls on five different phones. Stephanie hit my mind.

"Wonder what she wants?" I asked myself as I text her.

"Wusup, this Antonio." She hit right back.

"Wusup Antonio!!"

"Koolin... what on yo mind?" I shot that text, with intentions of cuttin through the chase.

"Can we talk??" She hit back. I waited about a minute or so, then I called her.

"Hey, wusup!"

"Heey Antonio! How you been doin?!"

"I been koolin! How bout you?"

"I've been doing great! Just working and taking care of my 2 daughters! You've been out... bout 3 years now and haven't even called me! Umm! I guess I would probably be the last one you would even want to talk to, but I understand. I do have an explanation if you want to hear it."

Stephanie was getting right to it! She already knows that if I hadn't contacted her after I was released I wasn't fucking with her. Shit, she left me high and dry!

"Antonio, I know you're still on the phone talk to me! We go back to the 5th grade!"

"That's what I was saying during that long-ass bid Step!"

"I know, I know! Just give me a chance to explain, will you?!"

I breathed a breath of exasperation being sarcastic before answering... "Okay... Explain."

"Not on the phone, meet me at the Ole Charley's restaurant downtown Sylacauga.

"Damn! Why so out of the way?"

"Because you know I'm married to Detective Garrison of the Birmingham Vice narcotics! Can you meet me or what?"

"Yea, I'll be there... give me an hour.

"I see you doing very nice for yourself these days!" Said Stephanie as she took a sip from her Apple Martini.

"Well baby, you know me! Been bout it."

"I know!! Right?! I like that car!" Said Stephanie, as she looked in the parking lot, referring to my all-Black Porsche Carrera.

"Its fly ain't it?" I said.

"Uh-huh! But look... I didn't get you down here to talk about your car."

"Yea, you ready to explain why you left me?" I said interrupting Stephanie. I smiled to put her at ease. She smiled back as she ran her hands through her hair.

"If it's difficult or something baby you don't have to worry about it."

"Nawl, nawl it's kind of, but it's not." Said Stephanie.

"Okay... I'm waiting."

"Okay... you remember when I used to ask you those questions like if I was pregnant would you want me to get an abortion or have it?"

"Yea... I remember. That was right during the time we broke up. I was telling you I wasn't with the abortion thing, and... and you said."

"If it's mine, I would want you to have it!" Said Stephanie interrupting me looking kind of agitated.

"On the strength of me saying that, did that hurt you?"

"You damn right it did!" Said Stephanie. "You don't remember I cried and told you that you was the only one I had been fucking!"

"Yea... I do now. I thought you was bullshittin!" I said.

"Well... I wasn't! I told you back then when I was asking you for the money for an abortion that you would remember this! Smiled Stephanie.

Now I'm getting spooked. "Wusup Step?"

"Well... when you got locked up, even though we had kind of got back together. I had in my mind what you had said to me about if it's your baby and all that. So... I went sour on you, but I'm not going to let that bother me and continue to keep your son away from you!"

"Son?!!" I said sitting there with my mouth and eyes wide open.

"Yea... son! I went to Chicago, where my grandfather is, and had him."

Stung by the news, I just sat there looking at Stephanie as she was gauging me to see my reactions.

"You playin," I said, a little too nonchalant for Stephanie's taste.

"Oh, you don't believe me?" Said Stephanie as she went to the pictures in her iPhone. "Look."

I grabbed the phone looking at a picture of a lil light-skinned, round-faced, semi-popeyed lil-boy. He had a flat nose, big lips, and a hairline like mine. I'm looking at features like my mama always said! He kind of looks like my nephew! Only one thing he had the slant and color of his mother's eyes which were almost hazel.

"He was 2 then." Said Stephanie as she grabbed the phone and slid it to some more pics. And handed me the phone. I was looking at pics ranging from ages 6 to 20. The older he got the more he was looking like me.

"Send these pics to my phone!"

"Why? You want to show them to your mama? To see what she think."

"Step, why you never told me? I mean, you straight left a nigga in the dark!" She got me so heated now that I'm almost getting loud with her.

"Because! You was on some bullshit like he wasn't yours! But I knew I couldn't do it forever!"

"So, when he asks where and who his daddy is, what you tell him?"

"I told him the truth!... That you was in prison and probably would be there for life!"

"That's fucked up Step!"

"I know, I know Antonio, but I was hurt! Especially, after I heard you had a baby by that skank hoe Sandra! Wasn't she on dope or something?!"

"Hell, hath no fury like a woman scorned," I said.

"Yea!! Whatever you want to call it!" Said Step, drawing the attention of other customers in the restaurant. "Sorry!" Said Stephanie, with an embarrassing smile on her face to me and the other customers.

"Well, I apologize for all that, but you still supposed to at least let me know about the baby even if you did leave me! Didn't think I was goin to get out huh?!" I said with an "uh-huh bitch" smirk on my face.

Stephanie rolled her eyes and smiled at this. "Thank god you did!"

"Already! So, is he still in Chicago or what? I want to meet him."

"No... he's in Birmingham, doing the same stuff that led you to prison! That's why I was glad we got this out the way, so you can talk to him!"

"Okay, so, where is he?" When I said that, like clockwork 3 young niggas, walked in the restaurant. The one in the front, was about 6 feet 2, about 250 lbs. with long dreads, mouth full of gold, and light-skinned. The one in the middle was short, about 5'7 or 5'8 light-skinned, kind of stocky athletic built like Dallas Cowboy running back Ezekiel Elliot, except with dreads and looked identical to me! My son! This nigga gangstafied, I said to myself. And the 3rd one, who was walking behind my son was a dark-skinned fellow, with a bald head, with diamonds in his ear, Rick Ross's beard, and Platinum teeth with crushed ice. The 2 fellows with him I gauged as his shooters.

"Wusup ma." Said D-Ant, which is my son who was looking at me with a shit-eating grin on his face. His grill gleaming like his shooters. I stood up and held my hand out to shake his hand as Stephanie stood up to introduce us.

"D-Anthony... meet your father Antonio... Antonio meet your son, D-Anthony.

"Wusup D-Ant!" I said enthusiastically. He hesitated for a couple of seconds before shaking my hand and saying, "I wanted to ask you the same thang!"

Chapter 18

Carlos had been laying low in San Antonio since he's escaped from witness protection. Well, not exactly escaped, but eluded his handlers. That's what made them put an APB out on him on the low. They just wanted him safe and alive but at the same time, they couldn't give a shit about him! It's just the fact that the Feds knew that Garcia stood a good chance of getting his conviction overturned. So, that means a new trial and they would need Carlos to testify again because he was the star witness in the first trial.

Agent Vinnie Testado was Carlos's shadow when he was in the witness protection. Agent Vinnie was adamant about locating Carlos, apprehending him, and have him placed in Federal Custody at a safehouse until this new trial is over. The Feds had been investigating the murder of Carlos's son since it happened and immediately started watching Garcia's immediate family. His wife, children, and all known associates past and present.

So far, they had nothing since they were flying under the radar. Their names had never been connected to any drug dealing so that was a plus, but something interesting happened one day. Some undercover agents had been dispatched to put Anita, Garcia's wife under heavy surveillance. They spotted this African American male having lunch with Anita in a downtown grill. The building in which her office where she ran her business was located. They took pictures of this guy and ran them through their database and a match was found! His name was Antonio Deangelo, an ex-convict with state and federal convictions for murder and conspiracy to possess and distribute cocaine.

Now turned entrepreneur, investor-business owner, CEO/owner of a hot record label, and suspected Kingpin leader of a violent drug-dealing criminal network ran out of Atlanta, Georgia. With this information Agent Testado immediately contacted the Georgia branch of the F.B.I. and D.E.A then informed them of what was going on in Texas and Mexico. Advised them to put a watch on Deangelo and associates. Agent Testado remembered what Carlos had said about it being a Black man who called his phone from his now-deceased son's phone. They had listened to the call themselves, but it was hard to authenticate a voice they've never heard before.

So now, Testado felt as if they had enough evidence now to put in an affidavit and submit a federal judge to get a wiretap on somebody's phone. Meanwhile, Testado has been hanging out in Dallas, Texas hoping that Carlos Desendez would surface there in revenge of his son's murder.

Carlos knew that since the trial most of Garcia's family and cartel had moved out of Houston. So now he was on a mission to find Anita and make her tell him who was the triggerman who took his son's life just before he slit her throat! He knew that Garcia was responsible, so he was going at his wife first! He knew what she was capable of. Even though he was a rat, he still had a few associates who would join him. Especially, if he was paying! Carlos still had money, so buying a few hungry wolves wasn't a problem.

Down in San Antonio, Carlos was getting a small crew of young wolves together that he met through his late son. With the help of one of his old acquaintances, he found out Garcia's youngest sister stayed in Dallas.

"We're headed to Dallas." Said Carlos after getting off the phone. They loaded up 4 deep in a Black 2017 Cadillac Escalade and sped off to the highway.

After chopping it up with my son D-Ant, I was amazed! This young nigga had his shit together. After I sat there for 2 hours with him giving my brief life story and explaining why I wasn't in his life all those years. He took me by surprise at how mature he was about the situation.

Of course, he had some anger, but he was really cool.

"Ain't no love loss... Pops!!" Said D-Ant halfway sarcastically with that sneaky grin.

"Shiiit! I say we lock this bitch down! The whole Southeastern region! S.E.C. Southeastern Conference. Let me in... Pops!

"Damn! Here we go!" I thought to myself. "This nigga going to be a handful." I gave him my number. "We'll talk," I said as I left the restaurant.

That night I caught a flight down to Baton-Rouge to watch a prospect for my agency. He was a Receiver who played with Grambling. After the Bayou Classic, I had dinner with him, his stepfather, and his fine ass mama. That I had been hooking up with on the low and fucking her brains out! That old nigga she had couldn't handle her relationship was purely a beneficial thing for her. Retired from the military, he got a good supervisor position at some upscale firm. Well, I'm pouring it on hard violating all kinds of ethical rules. Sliding big money to my prospect, gave him a fly ass drop-top Camaro and fly all through his mama! She was doing most of the enticing for her son to sign a contract with me and my agency so I can be his agent and get him in the N.F.L.! After kicking it and handling my business in Baton-Rouge I went on to Texas to kick it with my people... my plug Anita. I met her in a grill which is in a building in downtown Dallas where her office is located and had lunch. I hadn't got with her sister-in-law Conswela, Garcia's baby sister in a while. So, I called her up and it wasn't long before me and her was hooking up at my hotel room.

When Carlos arrived in Dallas, he got a suite in a hotel in downtown Dallas. Him and his young band of up-and-coming Guatemalan shooters. He called a few people which he used to deal with that he didn't squeal on. Trying to get information on Anita and her children.

"You fucking rat-snake. You've already taken down her husband and the whole empire! What more do you want?!" Said one of the old contacts. "Don't ever call my place of business or me as long as you live!" And then he hung up.

Shortly after the call, the old contact called Anita and told her what took place. With that info. Anita called up a couple of their old guns for hire for security measures. Then she called Antonio.

"Antonio, Carlos is in Dallas!" Said Anita.

"Oh yeah?! How do you know Anita?" I asked.

"One of my business partners in the exotic car business

called me and told me that Carlos called him asking about me. I had a feeling that he may pop up!"

"Okay Anita, do you have anybody around you?"

"Yes, and I have some more people on the way. I'm going to put a team together to find him!" Said Anita.

"Okay Anita, what do you want me to do? Me and Conswela are just about to leave my hotel room now." I said, as I was grabbing my keys and motioning to Conswela, Garcia's sister to move.

"Hey Anita, I need to know how this dude look!"

"I will send you some pics of our mutual business phones!"

"Okay," I said, as I was reaching in my pocket for that phone. We headed out the door and got on the elevator.

"Anita we're getting on the elevator, so give me a couple of minutes before you send the pic. Matter of fact I'll call you back from that phone."

"Okay Antonio, I'm going to call my son Renaldo in the meantime!" Said Anita.

"What's going on?" Asked Conswela, Garcia's sister.

"Anita said, Carlos, the man that ratted on yo brother was here in Dallas!"

"I wonder what he is doing here?" Said Conswela, with a worried look on her face.

"I don't know, but it seems to me he's been asking around about Anita and her whereabouts!"

That's when Conswela's hand flew to her mouth. "Oh my God!"

"What's wrong? You okay?" I asked.

"He knows he's not welcome around us! He's here for only one thing... And that's revenge for his son!"

I thought about what she said and it made plenty of sense. Since I'm the one who whacked his son and he knew that a black man sent him the message from his dead son's phone. I know he don't know me, but if I'm seen around Anita and the cliche then he might put two and two together. Then I'll become the hunted! I need to get strapped up! I'll call Renaldo when I get his picture from Anita. I was thinking like hell when we got off the elevator and didn't notice the four Mexicans walking through the lobby or that one of them did a double-take when he looked our way and noticed Conswela, Garcia's sister.

Carlos and his four-man crew entered the hotel lobby heading to their suite. After they did a little riding around Dallas, he got in touch with somebody back in Houston and they confirmed that Anita was in Dallas, Texas. Running a couple of car dealerships and other businesses. Carlos noticed this sexy Mexican female and black dude coming off the elevator. He did a double-take, not because this female was looking good. He knew who she was. She looked like Conswela, Garcia's sister.

"Mama mia'!" Carlos said to himself.

At that moment he noticed the black dude with Conswela looking at his phone as if he were reading a text or looking at a picture.

"Que esta pasando?" 'What's going on?' Asked one of Carlos's henchmen. He noticed how Carlos had did a double-take like he knew the Mexican woman or the black dude with her or both.

"Creo que la conozco?" 'I think I know her!' Said Carlos as he watched the couple walk out the door into the parking lot. He quickly changed directions and got on their trail.

"I believe that is her!" Said Carlos, more to himself than his henchmen as he exited the hotel and watched Conswela and the black man.

Shortly, valet parking pulled up in a Yellow Ferrari 458 which Conswela and the black man entered. Conswela was in the driver's seat.

"Who is that?" The young henchman asked again.

"Garcia's sister." Said Carlos as they went to retrieve their Escalade to follow them.

I was getting the pic of Carlos that Anita was sending as soon as I was getting in the car. By habit, I was looking around once I got in the car. I looked dead in this ratting muthafuckas face! Yes... like clockwork, I looked back dead in Carlos Desendez eyes as he was coming out of the hotel we were leaving. I'm thinking to myself "is this a setup?!" Then I quickly got that thought out of my mind because these folks were loyal! It just was a coincidence. I was looking in my mirror as we pulled off and noticed Carlos and his crew were running towards the parking lot as if they were going to follow us!

"Yo Conswela ... They following us." At least that's what it looked like. Conswela looked at me speechless. From my face to the road and back to my face.

"Who?!" She asked, looking as if she feared my answer.

"Carlos and about 3 more Mexicans." Actually, they were some lil treacherous Guatemalans who were guns for hire. With that Conswela kind of put, the peddle to the metal making that Ferrari do what it do. I was calling Renaldo and looking at the mirror at the same time. I didn't see any signs of them, but I still needed some iron and reinforcements!

"Si." Answered Renaldo

"Creo que esloy sienoz sequie'd!" 'I think I'm being followed.'

"Pov quien!" 'By who?" Asked Renaldo.

"Carlos Desendez!" The other end of the phone was silent for about 10 seconds. "You there?" I asked.

"Si! Where are you?" I told Renaldo which way we were traveling after Conswela took a couple of quick turns to elude any possible trails. I told him how we got spotted and how I knew it was him off the top. Once he realized his aunt maybe stands a chance of being in danger and that Carlos's presence here in Dallas wasn't by accident. That his presence was a threat, he was ready to react.

"Tell my aunt to come to Cole Manor. You all are close to that area now. Go to Hester Ave. and then go to these condos. The address and condo number are 69 C. House number 7."

"Okay... make sho you bring me firepower.

"Si." Answered Renaldo and he hung up.

I recited the address to Conswela as she put it in her Ferrari's GPS.

Chapter 19

Agent Testado of the Federal Bureau of Investigation had received information out of the Dallas office that Carlos Desendez had called around in the Dallas, Texas area seeking Anita Abregado.

"I knew it!" Said Agent Testado as he received the info. Carlos had called a number to this certain Mexican business owner in Dallas, Texas whose number was already tapped by the federal government on a separate investigation. When they monitored the conversation, they figured it was the missing government witness from a protection program in Montana. With that, they passed it on to Testado who had affidavits granted to tap and monitor calls to and from Carlos Desendez, Anita Abregado family and any associates who may raise suspicion related to said investigation.

Now he had bullets to fight with! So far, nothing came up on Anita except a few business-related calls on those phones in her business offices. Garcia's younger sister's phone had been monitored and they had a few texts and calls between her and Antonio Deangelo. The ex-con record label, business owner/ entrepreneur out of Atlanta. Possible head of an amoeba like network of drug distributors and suppliers with a home based in Atlanta, Georgia. From closely monitoring Conswela

Abregado's phone he learned she was at the Omni Hotel in downtown Dallas. They had been using iphones & smartphones so the GPS in the phones told on them.

"I wonder what Garcia would think if he knew this nigger was banging his sister!" Said Agent Testado as he sat in his undercover Malibu. He had the hotel under surveillance waiting on Conswela and Antonio to make a move. "There they are!" Agent Testado said to the interior of his car. He was alone but had back up on deck if needed.

They jumped in a yellow Ferrari... a new one! He immediately cranked up his car and got on their tail. If he would've waited just another 3 minutes, he would have possibly spotted Carlos Desendez.

"Fuck! This bitch lost us!" Said Carlos as he banged on the steering wheel of the Escalade. He was just 3 minutes behind Conswela in the yellow Ferrari until she started doing everything on the dash and taking all those quick ass turns. He was riding all over Dallas looking for that Ferrari. He didn't know if he had been recognized at least by Conswela, because she didn't even look his way but the black guy with her locked eyes with Carlos. It was almost by coincidence, but it seems as if the black guy had a look of recognition in his eyes! His gut instinct was telling him something.

"That could be the one!" Said Carlos.

"The one what?!" Said one of his shooters.

"The one who killed my son!" Then Carlos went back to the fateful night that he received the call. "Don't ever show back up in court!" Then, before that the video of his son being shot and falling back into a hole screaming. Plus, the video before that asking. "What did I do?!"

"Amigo watch out!!" Screamed one of the henchmen.

SCREEECH!!! Carlos stomped on the brakes just in time before almost hitting a Black 4-door Porsche Panamera at a red light. Carlos had done zoned out thinking about his son's murder and his possible murderer.

"Hey mothafucka, what the fuck you blind or something?!" Said the driver of the Porsche Panamera after jumping out with a chrome desert eagle in his hand. Carlos's young wolves immediately went for their guns, but he calmed the situation.

"Hold up!" Said Carlos as he motioned with his hands as if he were holding them back, "Me Disculpo mi ma! I apologize! That was my bad!" Said Carlos as he looked out the driver's window.

"Fuckin ass hole you almost got smoked!" Said the driver as he got back in the Porsche, but right before he was getting back in the car the young fly Mexican looked back at Carlos' mug and Carlos couldn't believe his eyes.

"It's Renaldo!" Said Carlos as the Porsche was speeding off from the red light. "Garcia's son!! An eye for an eye!"

Agent Testado had been cold trailing the yellow Ferrari for 30 minutes. The almost lost him! With the speed of the Ferrari and all the eluding turns, like she knew she was being followed! He didn't know if they did or not because he still had them in sight. He was going to catch up with them and see what they're up to. He's hoping that he bumps into Carlos here in Dallas, because he is about 90% sure that he might be here seeking revenge. He found out that Garcia had a wife, son, 2 twin girls and a younger sister here in Dallas.

"Mama mia!" Yelled Agent Testado as he read the info.

Coming through on his tablet, from the Feds Electronic surveillance men. They showed where Antonio Deangelo had made a call to Garcia's Abregado's son Renaldo indicating he was being followed by Carlos Desendez and Renaldo gave him an address to a safehouse for him and his aunt Conswela to meet him. Antonio told him to bring him some "Fire Power!" He wanted guns! A war was brewing right before his eyes.

He got on his walkie talkie and immediately got with his colleagues to get and set up some intense surveillance on Conswela and Antonio in hopes of killing two birds with one stone. Hoping that they would lead Carlos to them and they may make a quick arrest on Antonio and Conswela or at least get a reason to bring them in for questioning .The murder of Carlos Desendez Jr. is still unsolved and maybe this would re-open the cold case. Evidence in the case indicated that a black man sent Carlos Sr. a pic/video of the murder of Carlos Jr. The message from Carlos's phone said that a black man made a threat to Carlos Sr. about not coming back to court.

So now the feds and their tech people were trying to authenticate Antonio's voice and match it up with the recent call just made to Renaldo.

"If he said that he was being followed by Carlos Desendez, then you might be following Carlos!" Said one of the agents.

Agent Testado had called. "I thought about that too!" Said Testado.

"Just stay on the Ferrari and tech people will stay on their phones!"

So even if you lose her we'll relocate her!"

"Si." Said Testado as he hung up. "Everything and everybody are going to fall right into our hands if they fuck up!"

At a cool distance and pace Carlos was trailing Renaldo from another lane on the freeway. After Renaldo had sped off from the red light where Carlos almost ran into him and his Porsche. He turned right at the right light just as Renaldo. He can tell Renaldo wasn't really paying him any attention because he pulled off putting a phone up to his ear.

"That is Renaldo! Garcia's son!" Said Carlos. "I'll never forget that lil punk! Looks just like his father. A younger version." Carlos was telling young Lobo how he knew who Renaldo was.

Renaldo had added on a little speed as he took a turn and headed out to the freeway. Nevertheless, Carlos still was following him determined to retaliate for what they did to Carlos Jr.

"We have accidently run into 2 of Garcia's family members in this area! Someone lives over in this area or possibly got a safe house." Said Carlos.

"So, what you want to do? Keep following him until he leads us into an ambush?" Said Enrique, the leader of the Guatemalan's hit squad.

"I say we get him while we got him in sight." Said of the shooters from the back seat.

"Yea!" Said all three of them.

"No, no! We plan on getting away we got to be more subtle!" Said Carlos.

"I'm not going to prison!"

Renaldo got off the freeway and so did Carlos. They trailed him from the other lane until about 6 cars was between them, they switched lanes and got in the same lane as Renaldo. Renaldo took a quick right and rode that street for about 5 minutes. Took a left into a nice suburban neighborhood. A couple of minutes down that road. He pulled into a parking lot of some nice condos. Carlos kept riding until he noticed Renaldo getting out of the Porsche. Once he was sure which condo, he went into he stopped the truck. He slowly backed up and turned around and rode around the condos and he spotted the yellow Ferrari.

"Bingo!" Said Carlos.

Chapter 20

Back in Atlanta, Georgia shit was bout to get hot! One of Brainhead's partners, Larry T from Montgomery, Alabama had smoked a nigga by the name of Cee. Nobody actually knew what the beef was about, but Larry T rolls hard with a known young rapper by the name of Brainhead and them niggas still got shit on lock with the dope game. And to top it all off the nigga Brainhead is down with a rich nigga... Antonio Deangelo.

"Maan dis nigga is trying to extort us!" Said Brainhead as he was telling Antonio the story. "Da nigga say he wants 88 racks for his injuries! Larry T shoulda killed him!" Said Brainhead.

Antonio told him about his situation in Texas so Brainhead let Antonio off the phone.

Later on, Brainhead was riding on the Southside in his Cadillac and he noticed Cee getting out of a Black Maxima at this bootlegger spot. The way he was ducking in and out of the car it looked as if he was reaching for a gun. That's what Brainhead was thinking as he let the passenger window down in his new Cadillac XTS and started squeezing the trigger on his military issue P-89.

POP-POP-POP-POP-POP-POP

"Aah mufucka my baby!" Santisha screamed.

That was Cee's baby mama. Nobody got hit but the Maxima got sprayed so that's when the extra shit came in. Cee had got Brainhead's number from somebody.

"Eh nigga! My baby and baby mama were in the car!"

"Nigga I didn't know! You shouldn't have been flexin on me like you had a gun! What the fuck, you think I'm going to let you shoot me?!" Said Brainhead.

"Well, I wasn't going to shoot you, but now my baby mama is going to sign a warrant on you! Nigga you need to get 200,000 to me before 8 tonight or you going back to the joint." Said Cee before hanging up on Brainhead.

"Fuuuuck!" Hollered Brainhead as he looked at his phone. Brainhead called around until he got "Crawdad's" number, "Santisha's brother" trying to get him to talk to Santisha to no avail.

Brainhead was pacing the floor back and forth in his safehouse over in Buckhead as his crew sat back watching him.

"I say we go find them and make both of them disappear!" Said Brainhead's right-hand man, Dingo. With that, Brainhead stopped pacing and looked at Dingo.

"They're the victims and only witnesses and if there are some more witnesses, we'll find them... Asap!" Said Dingo. Dingo was older than Brainhead by 4 years, but he was super loyal to him. Brainhead smiled at this.

"Let's get it!" Said Brainhead.

They made a quick plan and piled into a Black van. They ducked off and rode out to find Cee and his baby mama. They knew where they lived so they went there and found out they weren't home. They quickly broke in and waited on them to come home. They sat there in Cee's house for about an hour.

Then finally, they came home.

"Don't' worry baby, we'll get them niggaz!" Said Cee as they entered their home. Santisha leading the way.

"Fuck dat red ass nigga going to pri...Aaah what the fuck!" Screamed Santisha as she discovered Brainhead sitting on their couch when she turned on the light. Just as soon as she was about to get the words out of her mouth, she was blindsided by a big ass .357 barrel across her head.

"Aye maan!" Screamed Cee as he was struck in the right temple with the butt of the rifle.

"Now... I tried to be diplomatic about the situation, but y'all wanna extort me, go to the police on me..."

"Heeelp!" Screamed Santisha, interrupting Brainhead.

"Shut up Bitch!" Said Brainhead as he kicked and stomped Santisha unconscious.

"As I was saying... Cee, you should've kept this in the streets!" Then with no warning Brainhead shot Santisha in the head and shot Cee in his head 3-times with the silenced 9mm. They wrapped their bodies up in plastic, weighted them down, and threw them in the Chattahoochee River.

Santisha had already signed a warrant on Brainhead so the police were looking for him and when the fed got a whiff of it. They immediately intensified their investigation by looking at any and all calls coming and going from Brainhead's phone. They were already dissecting their earlier conversation about what was going on in Atlanta and the little bit he revealed about his situation in Texas.

Now the feds were looking at the text from Brainhead's

phone to Antonio's phone. Brainhead text: "My problem is gone fishing in the Chattahoochee!" Antonio text: "Gud!!"

With that information, the fed and the locals were heading to the Chattahoochee River. Once Cee and Santisha 's family found out they were missing and possibly murdered due to all the blood the C.S.I had found in the house. Their brothers crewed up with some of their friends from the community and were looking for Brainhead.

Chapter 21

PROLOGUE TO A SHOWDOWN

Carlos and his goons had parked their Escalade around the corner from the condos where Renaldo, Conswela, and the black man were at. They were on foot dressed in black strapped with four assault rifles and ski masks on their head.

"Hey Amigos get ready!" Whispered Carlos as he pulled his ski mask over his face and his team followed suit. What Carlos didn't know was that Renaldo owned these condos. Had secret cameras installed all over within a block radius and the main monitor was in the condo where they met Renaldo.

"That's them!" Said Antonio as they zoomed the camera on a black Escalade with four Latin men getting out with rifles.

"Those are the same assholes who almost rear-ended me not far from the hotel! Holy shit! That's Carlos!" Said Renaldo realizing how close he was to death at the red light. He grabbed his phone and hit speed dial "Cua'n lejos stas de" 'How far is you from here?!"

"About two blocks!" Answered the man from the other phone.

"Hurry! Carlos and 3 men are closing in on foot dressed in black and driving a black Escalade!"

"We're on it!" Answered the sicario.

Renaldo got off the phone and gave Antonio a Black AK-47 and A44-Desert Eagle. Renaldo grabbed the same choice of weapons and led Antonio down a secret passage. Through the closet which led down to a secret door and exit on the ground level of the condos. Renaldo had the whole video layout downloaded on his phone, so he knew exactly where Carlos and his goons were. They were headed in the direction of the condo that they had just left with ski masks on their faces. Renaldo and Antonio crouched down and tried to ease up on them when the last goon spotted them out of his peripheral vision. However, before he could react Antonio had already raised up and put one in his head. PLOW!! That shot set off a stream of events all at once.

Agent Testado had followed Conswela and Antonio to a nice neighborhood to some condos. He circled the parking lot a couple of times to see where a good place would be to set up surveillance. As he was pulling out of the parking lot, he noticed a Black 4-door Porsche pulling in.

"Nice car!" Said Agent Testado as the Porsche passed him and then it hit him. "Renaldo!" He recognized Garcia's son from the pictures the agency had sent him. Not wanting to seem too obvious Agent Testado pulled out of the complex as if he was heading on his way. About 30 seconds out of the complex he passed a black Escalade as he was cruising looking for a way to pass back through the condos and set up surveillance. He called his colleagues through his radio and told them the address where the subjects were located. He took a side street and circled back to the condos. As he was coming back through the parking lot, he noticed the same black Escalade cruising out of the parking lot as if they were lost or watching somebody.

"Hmm... strange. They could be lost, or... could be stalking!" The police in him made him very nosey and observant. Then he thought about the intel he had so far. "Could be Carlos or cartel security." He said to himself.

Agent Testado cruised back through the lot in hopes of finding a parking space while looking back towards the condos at the same time. He pulled out and drove slowly up the road about half a block away from the condos. He noticed on a side street to his left that four men were moving slowly yet quietly, cat-like, trying to sneak up on someone.

Agent Testado backed up and slowly drove down the side street. Not wanting to drive into an ambush he called for a little backup. Due to suspicious activity happening in the vicinity of an ongoing federal investigation. Within 2 minutes of seeing the suspicious-looking men, a loud shot went off PLOW!!!

"Oh shit!" Said Agent Testado as he fumbled with his walkie-talkie. "Shots fired! Shots fired!" He screamed as he sped through the neighborhood heading back to the condos.

After Antonio dome checked the masked man, he quickly aimed the chopstick in the direction of the other 3 men and let off a volley of shots. FPLOW-FPLOW-FPLOW-FPLOW-FPLOW-FPLOW!! Downing another one before taking cover from return fire. PLOW-PLOW-PLOW-PLOW-PLOW-PLOW!!

"They're on the move!" Screamed Renaldo, as the return fire stopped, and the other 2 masked men took off running around the condos heading back out toward the parking lot.

"There they go!" Said Antonio as they spotted the 2 men coming from around an apartment and ducked down running towards the parking lot. They had the goons at an angle, and they quickly let off about 8 shots apiece spraying parked cars and all! Trying to kill whoever it is. Taking cover behind cars and running at the same time, the 2 remaining men from the hit squad were almost pinned down by Renaldo's reinforcements, who were pulling up in a Black Hummer. They knew it had to be someone from Renaldo's crew or the police because they didn't have any backup. So, when the Hummer pulled up fast and threatening. The retreating shooters immediately aimed their rifles at the Hummer and commenced dumping   at   it.   PLOW-PLOW-PLOW-PLOW-PLOW-PLOW!!

One of Renaldo's men in the Hummer caught one to the head, but the other 3 returned fire after regrouping. By then they had retreated to some thin woods which led to a group of houses on the street, bustin shots back at the crew in the Hummer at the same time. They made their way to the Escalade which was a couple of streets over.

As Agent Testado sped back to the condos in the direction he heard the gunfire erupt he knew what was going on. Carlos Desendez was in that black Escalade and had tracked down Renaldo or followed him to the condos and was trying to settle the score he had with the Abregados. Which was about the killing of his son Carlos Jr. Agent Testado was coming from the opposite street that he had left leaving the condos. That's the street that the Hummer with Renaldo goons came from. As he approached, he was met with heavy gunfire from Renaldo's people.

"Shiit!" Screamed Agent Testado reaching for his gun and returning fire. "Officer under heavy gunfire! I repeat, Officer under heavy gunfire!" Screamed Agent Testado into his walkie-talkie.

"We are on our way!" Said the agent on the other end of the walkie-talkie.

Part 3

When It Get Gangsta!!
"When it get gaangstaa! Mufuckas gone ride or die!"
Zero/Geto-Boys Da Foundation 2005

Chapter 22

"That was the fuckin feds!" Screamed Renaldo as they sat at the round table of one of his safehouses. His mother Anita, Aunt Conswela, and Antonio were there with him.

"I know them unmarked cars!" Said Renaldo. Renaldo was referring to Agent Testado as he pulled back up to the condos. His men opened fire on Agent Testado due to the speed and urgency that he induced on arrival. Either you're the enemy or the law!

Once Antonio and Renaldo recognized the police they retreated to the condos, got Conswela, and took the secret passage that led 2 blocks over to a mini-mansion that Renaldo owned. Once they left, within minutes, the whole area was flooded with feds, police, ambulances, and detectives.

"Antonio, we need to get you back to Atlanta!" Said Anita. "It might not be safe to take a plane from Texas. We need to get you back by car. Just in case."

"No doubt!" Said Antonio, Anita made a phone call and within minutes Antonio was being picked up by 2 Mexican women in an all-Black Cadillac XTS.

Chapter 23

1 YEAR LATER

Riding around Atlanta, Georgia in my all-white Maserati Quatro Porte and thinking about the shit that's been going on in these streets. The industry side of my life is all about the check with me! I'm not an industry nigga so to speak. Meaning I got more serious shit going on in my life within my circle. The first couple of days I got back in Atlanta the fucking Johnnie Law was hanging around my studio and office – Headquarters, for my music label.

They wanted to question Brainhead about some nigga who came up missing. The only thing they had was some blood at the house they were missing from. Plus, the fact they were already looking for Brainhead due to the warrant Santisha (Cee's girl) had signed on him about the shooting situation and a funky-ass text Brainhead sent me about somebody going fishing in the Chattahoochee River.

They questioned me, and I told them "Call my lawyer!" Long story short. They questioned me and Brainhead about the situation in the presence of our lawyers. Arrested Brainhead about shooting into an occupied vehicle, Santisha's warrant. That case eventually got dropped. They never found Cee's or Santisha's body so that was a cold case.

And last, but not least the Feds were questioning me about ties to the cartel which is operating out of Texas. Ties to Anita Abregado family shootings and killings of some Mexican cartel snitch's son in Mexico. The shooting of a couple of Guatemalans in Dallas and the attempted murder of a federal agent named Testado or something.

I knew nothing about it... at least that's what my attorney told them. "If my client isn't under arrest, may we leave now?!"

One of the agents, said something about some texts to Brainhead from me talking about a situation in Texas. Texts and calls from supposedly my phone to Renaldo Abregado's phone talking about some guns! They had nothing to really hold me on it seems, so they let me go. I made the headlines "Rap Label CEO/ Owner Questioned by the Feds". And all that type of shit. "Bossman and leader of suspected drug gang walks." That had the Feds hot as a hooker who would fuck on credit!

"Hey, Mr. Deangelo! It's not over!" Said one of the agents.

"Yea... right!" I said as I hopped into a stretch Cadillac with my lawyer looking like we were heading to a funeral! The Feds down in Texas had questioned Renaldo, but he came out clean... for now. He told me the Feds were looking for Carlos Desendez because he was spotted the night of the shooting in that area by an Agent Testado. We knew the heat was on, but we kept on Rockin!

Got new phones and were moving plenty of cocaine, heroin, and marijuana. My organization was game-tight on my end! All my partners and people who dealt with or under them were eatin!! Riding foreign cars and living in nice big houses! Living lavishly on dope money bred envy so we had a lot of enemies. Just as soon as 1 or a group of them let it be known and jump fly with us we jump time with them and straight wreck shop! Murder, kidnap, extort, make them leave town, or make them join the bird gang! Not baby's bird gang, but literally real birds! Way up there! Like one of my OG's from Opelika, Alabama used to say! On the industry side of my life, we were eating like Pac-Man!

My partner and flagship artist Brainhead was dropping CDs and mixtapes back-to-back! Doing shows all over the U.S. and overseas. The group ATL cartel was hot at the time with 2 new CD'S and touring. My R&B guy was doing big numbers rockin them women to sleep doing vocals and hooks for my artists and others.

But the one who was doing astronomical numbers and was quickly famous out of nowhere was the Drake-looking nigga from Houston Texas. He always had these lil twins with him, twin sisters! Every time I see them that future song come into mind... "Twin sisters". I wanted to fuck both of them, but the one who was a lil thicker and I could tell was probably the oldest. That's the one!

I catch some helluva vibes from these two though! Some fuck vibes, but also some dangerous death vibes!! Anyway, the nigga Jon-Jon could get on all levels with that Houston, Texas swag. He can get emotional with these bitches. He could talk that playa shit. He could definitely get gangsta-gutta wit it! Flashy fly ladies man, yet I'm bout that street shit! Robbery-murda, I take hits and flip bricks shit!

He was doing big stages! Madison Square Garden shit. My lil nigga Brainhead still didn't vibe with him! It wasn't hater shit, Brainhead didn't like him from the jump! He always said it was something about that nigga. I wasn't doubting my lil brother because we been in the trenches together. He got an official stamp of approval from me a long time ago!

I told him, I feel some shit from him and them lil hoes also. "I'll keep an eye on him," I said to Brainhead. As I was whippin my Maserati into the parking lot of my record label. I see Jon-Jon and his entourage gathered around a Black Lamborghini. A couple of them niggaz did have a shiesty look on their faces. Along with one of them twin hoes when I pulled up on them. Jon-Jon was smiling, but it seemed as if there's something sinister behind the smile.

"What it do my nigga?!" I said to Jon-Jon as I was getting out of my car adjusting my Glock .40 with the woodgrain grip on it. It was almost visible! I wanted these niggas to know that I was strapped just in case they were the enemy... also a test! When a person does shit like that in the company of likewise minds you will surely get a subtle response.

Just as I thought! Two of them dudes with Jon-Jon were almost clutching but one of the evil twins had snatched and almost upped on me! She kept it behind her back though!

"Damn!" I'm thinking to myself, "What's really going on with Jon-Jon and his crew! I approached Jon-Jon and dap him up.

"Already! Wut it do Boss Man!" Said Jon-Jon.

"Koolin my nigga! I like this Lambo!" I said as I walked up to one of the twins who was standing kind of on the side of Jon-Jon. "This you playa?" I said, sly way talking about the twin as if I was talking about the Lambo. Looking her lil sexy ass up and down as she was posing with her left hand on her hip with an "Oh yeah?" smirk on her face, "She looks fast and dangerous!" I said nodding my head towards the car yet my eye still on twin.

"Yea! She might be... If you ain't careful!" Said the other Twin. The one I peeped snatching her pistol on sly when I approached.

'I wonder what's her agenda???' I said to myself, as I smiled at her. She smiled back! "Yea that's me, Boss Man! Just copped it. You like it?" Said Jon-Jon trying to calm the lil tension that is in the air.

"Hell yea I like it! I need to take it on a long ride one day!" I said looking at the thicker twin.

"Yea... me too!" Said, twin. The thicker one was looking over her Fendi sunglasses at me.

"Shiit, maybe you and I can take it on a spin together!" I said with daring eyes staring into big twin's eyes.

"She don't travel with strangers by herself." Said the lil twin.

"You can ride too! You heard that song by Future, "Twin Sisters?" I said as I was walking off.

"Yea! Do you remember the video?" Said lil twin. Referring to the twins in the video setting up a lick.

"Yea! Damn baby! Is it like that?!" I said as I turned around smiling at her comment.

At that moment I noticed Jon-Jon kind of shushing her by shaking his head in disapproval. With that lil twin turned back around to their entourage. Before I turned around, I noticed big twin still peeping with lust in her eyes and I grabbed a handful of my dick and subtly shook it at her, and walked off towards my office. "They definitely can stand a watching," I said to myself as I entered my building.

Chapter 24

"This lil stupid bitch bout to pull the nigga coat-tail to what's really going on!" Said Jon-Jon, referring to lil twin's behavior in their last encounter with Antonio.

"That nigga trying to fuck! He ain't caught on to shit!" Said lil Twin.

"Don't underestimate that nigga! He done been through all types of shit!" Said Big-Lo, Faygo's uncle who is paying Jon-Jon for the hit on Antonio and Brainhead.

"Dat's what I'm saying, we can touch the nigga through Big Twin! He trying to fuck her!" Said Jon-Jon as he paced back and forth on the balcony of his new downtown condo. Big Twin kind of got a little squirmish off the comment as she sipped on her Hennessy.

"What? Why everybody looking at me? I ain't bout to fuck that nigga!"

"Bitch please!" Said lil twin. "It's written all over yo face! You my twin, I know you."

"Nawl you must want to fuck him?!" Said, big twin.

"Yeah! To blow his brains out, get this money and back to Texas!" Said, lil Twin.

"Look both of y'all can fuck and suck that nigga as long as

you dead his ass! Yah hear me?!" Said Big Lo in his New York accent!

"It's been a year! What, I got to do it myself?" Said Big Lo as he left out the door.

"I should've smoked that nigga in the parking lot that day! Said lil twin.

"Nawl too many cameras! It's all about getting away with it!" Said Jon-Jon.

"Aw fuck! You act like you done gone soft!" Said, lil twin.

"What the fuck you mean?! I'm a star now! Bitch you think I'm trying to get fucked up?!" Said Jon-Jon.

"Look!" Said big twin, "I'll set it up!" Calming tension in the air between Jon-Jon and her twin. I'll find a way to get him isolated somewhere. Then we can handle our business, and nobody won't know a thing! They won't have a clue as to who knocked him off!"

"Okay, hot-momma! Don't get all tender pussy on me and fall in love! Remember the mission!" Said, lil twin.

"Matter of fact I'm going with you!!"

"No the fuck you not!" Said, big twin.

"Hold it! Hold it! We going to sit down and plan this shit! We're going to get a strategy to get him and that nigga Brain-head." Said Jon-Jon.

Truth be told, Jon-Jon had got rich rappin on Antonio's label. When he was supposed to be there to knock them off! Once his stardom took off so fast Jon-Jon had almost forgotten about why he was in Atlanta!! He had made a selfish move with the rap thing so to speak. At the same time, it worked out for the better! He was living his dream by default.

In Huatulco, Mexico 9:00 pm Carlos Desendez had been

incognito a whole year after the failed hit on Renaldo. The Feds had been looking for him, but he managed to avoid being caught by going deep into Mexico. He wasn't a hell of a factor even though he was back to getting money. So, the Mexican government and the Federales weren't really sweating him and they can be bought! He was down in Oaxaca getting his hands on some ice and marijuana through one of his son's friends. He slowly created a drug distribution network and mini cartel within the year he had left the witness protection. He had spots in Austin, Houston, and Arizona where distributors & suppliers did their thang.

So, he had secretly built up an army and money. With an attitude of fuck it, he was ready to take Renaldo and his nigger friend to war! What he had planned would draw them out of the woodwork.

Back in Atlanta at 9:28 pm, I was sitting behind my big oak desk, in a big leather chair with my hand up to my chin. A sign of deep thought. In my main office for R.I.C.O Enterprises which is the umbrella that my businesses are under. Herewith me are my 6 lieutenants and my son is one of them. He's distributing the boy (Heroin), the girl (Cocaine), and loud (cush/weed) in Alabama. Chi-Chi my childhood friend was one, dealt strictly with cocaine. Sonny and his son Lamont handled everything. My lil Potna was my other lieutenant that handled all loud and midgie. Also, Brainhead had the security team and we called them the "Young Wolves". If they were sicked on you, yo ass was got! You had to be a sharp and mighty warrior to escape or defeat these lil creatures. Like Yo Gotti said, "I don't have goons I have creatures that are so hungry they'll eat ya!"

Brainhead and his squad would still put the T.S.I muscle game down even though he was famous. But it's mostly when some lil beef starts cooking from so-called rival crews. Our shit was like a hierarchy organized and structured but on a big level. I wasn't too interested in who ran this block, zone, or hood. Been there done that. I'm more into distribution and supplying not just one geographical area in the city, but throughout the united states!

The niggaz we serve got crews who got crews! Break it down like this! I'm the head, the chief executive-owner-boss, the kingpin, and all of that! My next in command is my childhood friend "Chi-Chi". He was Capo! Even though I dealt with my other lieutenants exclusively, he sometimes made sure their supply was in their hands-on time and all money was turned into him. My nigga was super paranoid and careful, so it had got to a point that nobody got work straight out of his hands 85% of the time or put money in his hands. He had a web of young pretty women doing all the transactions and meeting people, etc.

Me and that nigga always had a way with women, so they weren't hard to recruit. They wanted to be a part of something and fuck us, so we put them to work. But nevertheless, they got paid well!

My son, of course I made a top lieutenant once I found out he was thorough as his pops and he ain't scared to bust that hammer. He was in Birmingham selling everything from bricks and pounds to rocks and sacks! He had trap houses all over the city organized too! He had 2 niggaz to a trap handling the sack and guns, plus lookouts strategically placed on his blocks. He had out of towners all over Alabama coming to buy our product! He had a few of his childhood crew back in Chicago hustling good. He knew a few niggaz coming out of Alabama prisons who were good rappers. He started a record label that was exclusively distributed through my record label, R.I.C.O Entertainment.

At first, his only problem was his stepfather. Detective Larry Garrison of Birmingham narcotics. He had been stepping to my son on some threat type of shit. I called Stephanie and told her to get that nigga in check before it be a man down! It wasn't long she was giving that nigga a duffel bag with half a million in cash! He was officially on the team! Bought! My baby mama, Stephanie had a lot on that man and besides, he could use the money!

"You get the other half in a week!"

"Stephanie, what's this?" Asked Detective Garrison, Stephanie's husband.

"You'll receive further instructions later... as for now... stay off of my son and let me know what you hear!" Said Stephanie and walked out of the bedroom. She had him by the balls! She had just walked down on him fucking some young high school girl. One of her daughter's friends.

I had another $500,000 for him. He will be our inside plug to let us know what's happening. I already had one up here in the A. A chick I grew up with I called Apple. She used to suck my dick with a green apple now and later back in 88'. We had a lot of out-of-town traffic and plus we were putting down out of town!

Each one of my lieutenants had someone govern somebody out of state with our product. Not just a seller and buyer relationship. I'm talking like a director over a manager who has employees under them! For example, Sonny might have his nephew in Phenix City, Alabama with some niggaz selling grams, 8 balls, and quarter ounces of coke and crack. He might have another nigga in the same territory with half ounces, ounces, and half of a big or eighth (2 ounces and a quarter). And another hustler with strictly 4 ½ ounces (eighths), quarter keys (9 oz.) and halves (1/2 of a key) and his nephew handled all bricks (keys) with each lieutenant with at least 7 or 8 governors under them. Who in turn got a couple of managers under them with fire products at all times!

We were getting military duffel bags of money, literally! Like Tony Montana and his crew on Scarface when they were going to the bank. "Push it to the limit!!" When they were going to have major problems in their respective town, turf, city or etc. We send in the young wolves!!

Anyway, while me and my lieutenants-potnaz were sitting here discussing business my secretary hit me at my desk phone.

"Wusup Cynthia?!"

"Were you expecting a visitor?"

"No, I'm still in a meeting."

"I know! But this young lady here is adamant about seeing you! Said she drove from South Carolina."

"Damn! Who the fuck could this be?! Ask her her name."

"I already have her name. Her name is Kadia!" Said Cynthia.

"Damn!" I told myself. "Yo let's end this meeting. So, I can see what's up."

Everybody left out of my office and in came Kadia.

"You haven't been answering my calls or Facebook messages?!" Asked Kadia.

"It's good to see you too Kadia."

"I want to know what happened to my cousin?!"

"What you mean?!" I asked, playing dumb.

She was speaking on her cousin Brad, who tried to play me a couple of years ago. Them boys are catfish bait at the bottom of the Chattahoochee River I wanted to say.

"Nigga you know what the fuck I mean! My cousin was dealing with you when he came up missing. Now all of a sudden that scrub ass nigga Ricardo who used to work for Brad is supplying the city!"

"What do I have to do with that?"

"What you got to do with it? The nigga been getting work from you!! The word on the streets up my way is that Ricardo set my cousin up for some Atlanta niggaz who he supposedly owed? Do that ring a bell?!"

"Nawl, I don't know nothing bout that!" I said.

"That's a lie Antonio because I'm the reason you started fronting him dope in the first place!"

"Look Kadia, calm down!" I said.

"Calm down?! You need to be telling me what happened to my cousin!" Said Kadia.

Now the wheels in my head are turning! "Look... I don't know what happened to your cousin, but I will help in any way you might need me." I said in a calm way.

"Okay... This is the way you want to play?!" Said Kadia as she was walking toward the door. I just shrugged my shoulders at her. "Alright." Said Kadia as she walked out of the door.

"Damn!" I said as I sat down in my big leather chair. All the time I didn't know that conversation as well as the conversations held by me and my lieutenants were recorded.

Chapter 25

DEA Agent Captain Scott Thornton
FBI Agent Jeffery Mathers
FBI Agent Testado

"Wow! Who was that chic?" Said FBI agent Jeffery Mathers. "Call our surveillance men and tell them to follow the real fine chic with the white capris and green & white striped shirt!"

"Got ya," Said one of the Tech agents.

"Someone is missing!" Said Testado. "That's certainly the same voice on Carlos Desendez's phone the night of his son's murder. The same voice was recorded in Texas making calls to Renaldo Abregado about bringing him some guns because they had seen Carlos Desendez." Said agent Testado as if he were proving his case.

'The son of reputed drug cartel leader Garcia Abregado who Antonio Deangelo did federal time within Ft Leavenworth and Terre Haute where they got caught up in a race riot together." Stated FBI agent Jeffery Mathers proving that the

Georgia Bureau of Investigation(GBI) had been doing their homework.

"As a favor for helping Garcia and having his back during the riot, he plugged him once he got out" Said DEA agent Captain Scott Thornton.

Antonio Deangelo is somewhat doing the footwork for Garcia's cartel because they were nearly defunct. He still has his son who was flying under the radar, but he's always had his hand in! Antonio is working the eastern seaboard with Abregados' drugs and in turn, created his own organization. "We need to find out who this woman Kadia. Where she's from and who's missing. So, all the people who were in the meeting with Mr. Deangelo are the top dogs in the organization?" Asked agent Tostado.

"Yes! These guys are business owners, rappers, and rap label owners with heavy ties to the streets that are responsible for heavy drug trafficking, contract killings, and just plain old killings.

"In fact, Antonio Deangelo's right-hand man Chris Chee-Chee Floyd was on a murder case with Deangelo's computer networking programming company. Extortion, illegal gambling, and all of them are in the conspiracy." Said, agent Mathers.

"We just got to get a little more concrete evidence and connect all the dots and I say bring down an empire! We need to get this list they kept speaking on! Antonio had the list and he was asking questions and talking numbers. Referring to different people who govern someone with their drugs in another town, city, or possibly another state. Fellows look like we have a widespread conspiracy on organized crime! And check it out, the name of their organization is R.I.C.O!!! Just the act we have on our hands under federal law... R.I.C.O" said DEA agent Captain Scott Thornton. "And an 848-engaging in a continuing criminal enterprise...kingpin statute!"

Chapter 26

At the album release party, Jon-Jon's new cd was the who's who in hip hop and also the streets! Bad thots, groupies, and just plain old bad bitches were wall to wall! You even had a few r&b chics in the building...You also had the feds there too!! Undercover niggaz who were dressed and looking like thugs, rappers, and dope boys. Straight police, Antonio, and his crew were in the building deep! His label staff members, rappers on the label, singers on the label, and a lot of the street crew were there too! All of them were wearing black T-shirts bearing the name R.I.C.O Ent.

Chains flooded with flawless diamonds, charms and medallions were everywhere. Some had their medallions iced out with the name R.I.C.O In the VIP and all over the club the niggaz were shining in the dark! The women were working overtime trying to get under these ballers! The undercovers were taking pics with their phones and forwarding the pictures to emails of lead and head investigators that were building a case on this organization led by ex-convict Antonio Deangelo.

Speaking of Antonio Deangelo, the feds had planted a couple of fine-ass women on him, but it was hard for them to get next to him. Besides, a couple of big-ass ex-football players that were bodyguards and henchmen. There were these lil sexy ass twins that Antonio was sitting between and he was all in one of their ears! It seems like he was trying to fuck!

Fuck around I fuck yo twin sister "Twin sister" Futures song blasted in the background as big twin ground her ass all up on my dick as we danced in the middle of the dance floor. Well, gangstas don't dance we boogie, because all I was doing was holding my arms in the air. Grooving like back in the '90s on "I get around" except, I had a big bottle of Ace of Spades in my right hand.

"You done fucked around and got my dick hard!" I said as I leaned over into the twin's ear.

"Oh yeah?" said twin with lust in her eyes.

She sho nuff started working it like Rihanna! How she was backed up against Drake in that work, work, work video. I'm glad my girl wasn't there! It would be pandemonium by now.

"I'm going to fuck this lil bitch tonight," I said to myself. The other twin was right next to us putting that lil sexy ass on my partner Chee-Chee...Yet she was looking in my eyes biting her bottom lip making me want to fuck her!" I don't know if they will do menage' et trois with a nigga, but it sho was on my mind!

I don't know if I should try it, because there's something sinister about lil twin that I can't put my finger on. My alarms have been going off about their whole lil squad so I'm going to be careful and aware around them even though Jon Jon is one of my best-selling artists. I'm not comfortable around his crew. That's why when I get ready to fuck big twin there's going to be a young wolf or two in the vicinity securing the perimeter entrance and exits. They're some little women, but I recognize treachery and viciousness in both of them. Yet, thinking with my dick I just got to see what that hitting that pussy would be like! Usually, crazy or super devious women have some of the best pussy.

"Aye, let's bust a move! I said in the big twin's ear.

"Bust a move" meaning? Said twin being sarcastic yet leaning her mouth over her shoulder about to kiss me and she answered. A lil sexy seductive bitch!

"Let's go fuck!" I said cutting through the chase. At that, she reached back and grabbed my dick.

"You ain't fucking me in no bathroom!" said twin trying to stick to her plan, but all the time she would've fucked me right there on the spot!

"Nawl shawty I wanna get buck naked and stretch your lil ass out and get in all that pussy" I said as I squeezed her ass through her short tight leather Gucci dress.

"Let's go" said twin grabbing me by the hand to lead me out of VIP. Then

as if she forgot something she stopped in her tracks. Hold on, bae I'll be back then she turned around and went to holler at her twin who was already on us. I went and hollered at Brainhead.

"Yo check it out, finna go and fuck this lil broad," I said. He looked and saw who I was referring to and started smiling and shaking his head.

"Mann...you better watch that hoe bruh!!!

"I got her but, this is what I need you to do... Round up a couple of the young wolves. Get them to trail me and camouflage themselves to the point if someone else is trailing me they can peep it.! You feel me?"

"Okay, okay I got you bruh!" Said Brainhead.

The whole time I had my eyes on twin, her sister, and also the lil crew they rolled tight with even Jon. They were watching me on the low.

"Is one of these niggaz fuckin this lil broad or what?!" I thought to myself.

"Let's roll," said twin as she made her way through the crowd. As soon as we walked off Brainhead pulled up on one of our young wolves and put him up on game. Within seconds of me and twin walked out of VIP, 2 of them lil niggaz was cold trailing us and texting 2 more to meet in the parking lot.

Within that same moment, lil twin and Jon Jon was sitting on the couch engaged in deep conversation.

"What she say?" asked Jon-Jon.

"The bitch says she is going to text me and let me know what's up?" Jon-Jon sat there bouncing his head to the beat his fingers on his chin as if he's in deep thought then he smiled.

"She wanna fuck the nigga anyway, but if he ain't clear to be knocked off tonight it's still a plus. He may like the sex and start trying to fuck her heavy ya heard?!" With that said lil twin rolled her eyes really seething on the inside because she's frustrated. She wanted to be in her twin's shoes getting fucked tonight by a boss with the opportunity to body bag him. Mixed with a little jealousy lil twin was a ticking time bomb!

"She needs to text me and let me know their location, his ass dying tonight." Jon-Jon smiled at lil twin because he knew she was down with the murder game. He also knew when she felt lust and he knew that she was jealous her sister was chosen instead of her because she was also attracted to Antonio. He had grown up with the twins as nothing but friends, so he never fucked them. He always fucked their friends and they've always made money together. From selling candy in school, selling crack sacks, setting up robberies of big boys to straight out killing together so we had a bond.

"Well, when she sends a text let me know and then we'll go from there. Don't get gung-ho on me and try to carry this shit out yo self!" That's exactly what she had in mind! Jon-Jon knew it because she'd done it before out in Texas and almost got all of them jammed up.

"Okay...I'll try to," Said twin.

"Naw!! Ain't no I'll try it's I'm not going to!" Said Jon-Jon. Little did Jon-Jon know lil twin had already text Kabo a lil nigga in their entourage and told him to follow big twin and Antonio and that's where she fucked up!

Chapter 27

"Splack-splack-splack-splack." That's the sound of me and big twin's sweaty bodies colliding. I'm hitting this pussy from the back with her face down and ass up. Her back was arched, and she was throwing it back just like when she was dancing up on me. Twin was trying to out fuck me!

"Damn you can do it wit a dick in you!" Referring to what I asked her on the dance floor.

"Uh-huh!" Moaned twin. "Nigga I'm from Texas" she moaned. I got on my toes and started gangsta fucking her and pulling on her long weave. As I was about to bust off, I pulled my dick out and went straight to her mouth. I was straight porno style status as I pulled my cumming dick out of her mouth and started jerking it in her face then I told her.

"Bitch, I don't play!" She grabbed the sheet on the bed and wiped her face. Looked me in my eyes and put my dick back in her mouth again. She got me back right again in no time. Shawty had a mouth game like she could suck a golf ball through a hosepipe and she had some good tight pussy! I pulled out of her mouth, reached down, and grabbed her by the ankles. Then I spread her legs back and got all in that pussy using the straight pound game! My phone kept vibing on the nightstand and so was hers. Somebody was blowing us up, but my phone had the most activity. I grabbed the mu-fucka and cut it off, she did the same.

"Damn, this stupid bitch done cut her phone off!" Screamed lil twin.

"She must be enjoying herself some good dick!" Said Jon-Jon.

"Kabo had called me and told me that they were at a hotel on Biscayne called the Vagabond." He supposed to be calling me back and letting me know what's up and now he ain't an-swering." Said lil twin. She was pacing back and forth in the VIP.

"Sit down and have you a drink! You making me all ner-vous and shit!" Said Jon-Jon.

"Nervous? I ain't nervous I'm just ready" Said lil twin as she lit her 3rd straight Newport within 20 minutes.

"Yo sister knows how to handle herself and I told you it may not be easy to knock him off tonight. Big twin is up un-der him fa sho!"

"Nigga you trying to be funny!" Said lil twin as she sat back down and turned up a shot of Cuervo-silver.

"Naw...it's facts, we or she can catch him wit his drawers down for real. Literally or figuratively speaking ya dig?" Said Jon-Jon.

She felt where Jon-Jon was coming from, but lil twin was also thinking about Kabo.

"This nigga won't answer his phone and now it's off!" Said Tremaine, one of the young wolves. They had this nigga named Kabo tied up with tape around his mouth in the trunk of a white 2016 Chevy Malibu. Brainhead had told them to follow Antonio, watch his back and pull up on anybody who may pose a threat! They had noticed that when they met in the parking lot a nigga out of Jon-Jon's entourage came out of the club looking around trying to spot somebody. So they had two of the young wolves go ahead and follow Antonio and the twin. While they sat back and watched the nigga Kabo jump in a black Impala to follow Antonio. Then they in turn followed Kabo. Once Antonio pulled in at the Vagabond Hotel in Biscayne. Then noticed Kabo watching him and twin get out of the blue Lamborghini Aventador.

"Is this nigga fucking the lil hoe or what?" Said Tremaine.

"I don't know but it seems like the fool is watching them for somebody. The feds or somebody else." Said Lanski.

"You're right! Said Tremaine. Let's go check the nigga out!" They eased out of the car and headed towards the Impala. Kabo was too busy texting somebody and watching the hotel entrance to even notice Lansky and Tremaine approaching him until it was too late.

"Nigga, what the fuck you doing?" Said Lanski as he pointed the Desert Eagle at Kabo's head.

"Don't even try it, partner!" Said Tremaine as he approached from the passenger's side of the car pointing a Glock .40 at Kabo.

"Nigga get out!" Said Lanski as he grabbed Kabo.

"Hey man, hold up!" Said Kabo.

"Nigga hold up!" Said Lanski before hitting Kabo on the side of his head with the Desert Eagle. Kabo tried to run which ended up fruitless because Tremaine had shot the clips up under him and to the ground he went. They delivered a quick beat down before anyone could notice. Took him to the Malibu while putting tape around his mouth then tied his hands and threw him into the trunk and pulled off. That's when Lanski called Brainhead and told him what was going on.

"Call that nigga and tell him what's going on! Interrogate the nigga and find out what's happening with him. Who he's working for whether he's just freelancing!" Said Brainhead.

"Kid...You must not have heard what I said. This nigga is part of Jon-Jon's entourage plus he's sporting one of them chains with the 3rd on them!" Said Lanski, referring to the chain that Kabo had on and everybody in Jon-Jon's entourage wore which represents the 3rd ward in Houston, Texas.

"Ooh, my bad my nigga. I see where you're coming from. Come back to the club and get me. Text me once you're here" Said Brainhead.

"Bet!" Said Lanski as he hung up. He called Antonio's phone 5 or 6 times back to back and still no answer. He text the phone and told him the developments.

While Lanski was texting Antonio's phone and filling him in on new developments. Two undercover feds that looked like rappers/thugs are emailing and texting the lead investigators on the case about Antonio Deangelo and his crew's new developments! Once Antonio and the twin left the club the 2 fake thugs were trailing them until they noticed other people were trailing them also that was part of their entourage. So, they discreetly took pictures and fell back so they won't be noticed. That way they followed everybody who was following Antonio which led them into witnessing a kidnapping.

"Let's roll," Said the agent with the dreadlocks.

"Naw, hold up," Said the other agent as he grabbed his partner's arm.

"Hold up" This is a kidnapping in progress! What you mean?" Said the dreadlocked agent.

"Let's see how things unfold before we blow our cover. We'll follow them then take them down and arrest them."

The agents followed the white Malibu back to the club and watched as the rapper Brainhead got in the car with the guys who kidnapped a man.

"Man, you believe this shit!? Said the agent with the dreads.

"Yeah, these aren't just regular rappers, these dudes actually are gangsters." Said the other agent as he was taking pictures of the rapper getting into the white Malibu with the two men who just kidnapped a man from the parking lot of the Vagabond Hotel on Biscayne avenue.

"Them dudes are part of their entourage!" Said the agent with the dreads.

"Them niggaz got on them same black t-shirts with R.I.C.O Ent!"

"Right," Said the other agent as he fell in traffic behind Brainhead and the young wolves. Exercising their training on cold trailing suspects.

After getting my second nut I grabbed my phone, clothes, strap and went to the bathroom. After I cleaned myself, I was checking my phone and I imagined twin was too because her phone was blowing up also. After reading the texts that Lanski and Tremaine had sent me I immediately called them.

"Bout time my nigga!" Said Lanski.

"Now what you was saying?" I asked referring to their texts."

"Man, we got this nigga out at the swamps torturing his

ass. Aye bru, I told you to watch them hoes and that nigga Jon-Jon who is a snake." Said Brainhead. He had snatched the phone from Lanski when once he found out it was me on the other end.

"Damn!" I said.

"Man, they were supposed to knock me and you off for big Lo a year ago." Said Brainhead. " I done pistol whipped this nigga to a pulp! He'll tell me where his folks keep the family jewels at now! Look... I ain't goin to give him no chance to tell on me so you already hip! All these alligators! Man, what the fuck?" Who is that?" I heard Brainhead ask.

"Freeze motherfuckas!!"

"Shit!" Said Brainhead and after that: pop-pop-pop=pop, boom, boom, boom!!!

Then the phone went dead or he hung up and at the same time on my end "psst, psst, psst". I heard the sound of a silenced pistol and I dove in the shower inches from getting shot! Then I heard the door of the hotel room bust open along with a volley of shots. "Placka, placka, placka, placka!"

"Hoo now!!" I heard a voice with that Alabama slang. I knew it was the young wolves!

"Oh, now I answered back. They came to the door and I opened it up.

"Let's get out of here!" Said one of the young wolves. Two of them had been assigned to stay around the hotel. Long ago I had texted my location and room number to Brainhead who hipped the young wolves to my location.

What I saw when I stepped out of the room confirmed my intuition a while ago. Something was up with Jon-Jon, these twins, and their entourage. Big twin was laid out sideways swiss cheesed from her head to her feet and a pink nine millimeter with a silencer on it in her hand aimed towards the bathroom door. Next to her was her evil lil twin with a pink and black nine with a silencer on it! My people had shot some other lil nigga at the door that came with lil twin. We took the stairs to avoid any onlookers or potential witnesses. With a city like Miami, I think everybody tried to mind their own business, but the cameras are going to be a problem.

Just as we got to the 1st floor from the stairs fucking police lights were everywhere! People were flooding the lobby trying to evacuate that place due to the violence that had just erupted up on the 6th floor. We quickly mixed in the crowd and made it to the parking lot and lo and behold it was some old woman talking to the police and looking in our direction. We kind of split up in the midst of the crowd taking advantage of the nearly chaotic scene. Cars were pulling out at a rapid pace before the police could get deep enough to cordon the whole scene off. I hurried and took advantage of that situation and hopped into my Lambo, got on Biscayne, and made my escape.

Unfortunately, for my young wolves, the old white women had identified them entering the lobby in a hurry. Walking in after lil twin and the young nigga which to them looked suspicious. Then after the shots, they're hurrying through the lobby with another man. That's what they were doing when we entered the parking lot... Filling the police in! The police zeroed in on them and pulled them over!

"Damn!" I said to no one in particular as I'm thinking about not only what just happened, but what the fuck I heard when I was talking to Brainhead!

Chapter 28

"Man, this don't look good!" Said the dreadlocked agent, as they cold trailed the young wolves and Brainhead in a white Malibu with a kidnapped man in the trunk.

"We might need to call some backup!" Said the dreadlocked agent.

"You may be right, but before we do that let's see exactly where they're headed." Said the other agent.

He knew that would be the proper protocol in this type of situation, but he wanted to be a possible hero! " 2 local FBI agents working out of the Miami office derail a kidnapping in the midst of an ongoing R.I.C.O investigation".

"Hey, they're turning off the road heading towards the swamps." Said the dreadlocked agent snapping his partner out of his fantasy.

"I'll ride past the turn and turn around further down the street." Said the other agent. Once he turned around, he turned the lights off as he approached the road the young wolves had turned onto. After they turned on the road they killed their engine. They quietly exited the vehicle and walked down the dark road. Once they got a little closer they saw the white Malibu parked with the engine idling.

"Who da fuck you working for nigga!?" they heard a voice ask.

"I told ya man...Jon=Jon and the twins!"

"Whop!!" Brainhead was hitting the dude with the pistol again as he sat on the ground with his hands and feet tied together.

"Let's go, man!" Whispered the dreadlocked agent.

"Hold on!" Said the other agent. They had heard the kidnap victim explaining what he knew about a contract killing a guy named Big Lo supposedly was sponsoring. The contract was supposed to be on Antonio and Brainhead. Then one of the other young men was talking on the phone when Brainhead snatched the phone from the other guy and started telling the caller what was going on. When they heard the rapper Brainhead say something about some alligators, they knew what that meant! They had witnessed enough and they weren't about to stand there and allow the kidnap victim to be murdered and fed to some alligators! They both looked at each other, nodded, and sprung into action.

"Freeze motherfuckas!!" Screamed the dreadlocked agent.

"Man, what the fuck?!! Who is that?!" Said Brainhead.

At that moment, Lanski and Tremaine were reacting! Shoot first and ask questions later, but the dreadlocked agent was quicker.

"Pop-pop-pop-pop" catching Tremaine with three of those shots. Brainhead and Lanski quickly took cover and returned fire.

"Boom-boom-boom-boom-boom-boom!" 4 of those shots caught the dreadlocked agent. Two of those shots went into his head and the other couple of shots caught the other agent.

"Agents down! 2 agents down from gunshot wounds. I'm on...Aaaah!" Screamed the wounded agent when Brainhead stepped on his hand smashing the walkie-talkie with it.

"Fucking pigs!!" Said Brainhead. Alligators eat pigs too." Said Brainhead just before shooting the wounded agent in the head.

"Boom"

"What about this nigga?" Said Lanski speaking about the kidnap victim Kabo.

"Boom" "That's what's up with him!" said Brainhead after shooting him in the head.

"Let's throw these motherfuckas in the swamp." Said Brainhead. They grabbed the agents first and threw them in. It seemed as if the gators smelled the fresh blood because by the time their bodies hit the water you could hear the gators' mouths snapping on them! They threw Kabo in next with the same result.

"Damn, man we can't do Tremaine like that!" Said Brainhead.

"If we leave him here the alligators are still going to get him!" Said Lansky.

"Well fuck it we ain't gone throw him to them though! Let's get out of here."

3:30 AM...riding through coconut grove Miami after I escaped the scene at the hotel. I didn't even go back to the club I was riding in, a rental MKS Lincoln my cousin out of Opa-Locka had rented for me. Before my arrival in Miami, I had been calling Brainhead's phone for an hour and suddenly he called me.

"Wassup bru! Find yo way to coconut Grove and call me!" I Said.

"Bet!" After hanging up the phone I called my partner hamburger brother lil Noid to see if he could duck me off for a minute and just to my luck he could. I put the address in the GPS and headed out to Stewart Avenue.

The crime scene looked like something out of a Scarface movie or something.

"These girls are twins at least that's what it looks like!" Said one of the homicide detectives at the crime scene of a triple homicide at the Vagabond Hotel on Biscayne. The CSI was dusting the room for prints and any DNA.

"The kid up by the door got it right where he is laying!"

"What does that medallion on that chain say?" Asked one of the homicide detectives.

"3rd," Said one of the CSI workers as she stood and took a picture of the dead body.

"It was a big album release party over at the club LIV.

"He may be part of one of those rapper's entourage," Said a Cuban homicide detective.

"Google it, Maria," Said a Cuban homicide detective to a female detective.

By then some FBI agents burst into the hotel lobby flashing their badges and walking as if they were going to take over the crime scene.

"Special agent Hernandez of the organized crime investigations for the FBI. Who is the lead investigator here?"

"Me," Said the Cuban homicide detective.

"Detective Roberto Sosa". They shook hands.

"The FBI and the DEA have an ongoing investigation out of the Georgia and Texas office on some people who were in town at club LIV. We have a strong belief these people are involved with some of the people who are being investigated. Let's look back at the cameras till we can see things clearer. We may make some connections with the vics and their killer or killers!" Said the FBI agent.

6:38 AM

South Coconut Grove, Miami

"Maan... you got to be just fucking wit me!" I said to Brainhead as he was running everything that had happened down to me. As we sat in lil noid's safehouse smoking exotic.

"That shit a trip, because while y'all was getting raided I was getting shot at and almost got hit by the evil twins!"

"I told you that you better watch them hoes and I knew that bitch ass nigga Jon-Jon was up to no good!" Said Brainhead.

"Bru...we need to find that nigga now and murk his stupid ass! Then go to Atlanta and get that nigga Big Lo before he can do anything. We got to see if the police are looking for a nigga! I'm sure the law is looking at video surveillance and will see me and twin heading to the room!"

Brainhead looked at me and shook his head. "Damn bru!!"

"Rewind that again!" Said the lead FBI agent out of the Miami office. Agent Hernandez was pulling twin and Antonio's image up close for the 9th time. Running their images through the NCIC database. The female's name was Ranshika Miles and she has a small record. Felony convictions on assault 2 and obstruction of justice which was dealing with a murder and possible robbery out of Houston, Texas. Her identical twin also had a rap sheet for possession of heroin, assault 1st, and a couple of pick-ups for suspicion of murder. Now the guy, according to our offices out of Atlanta, Ga and Texas is the main star of the investigation. His name is Antonio Deangelo! According to our offices & comrades in Atlanta, he is a rap label owner, big businessman, and head of a violent drug gang by the name of R.I.C.O Entertainment! He's into heavy drug trafficking like the distribution of heroin, cocaine, crack, and marijuana. Based on evidence out of the Texas office, he is exclusively a possible drug lieutenant and hitman(muscle) for the Abregado Cartel that operates out of the Dallas-Houston Texas Area"

"We had been getting emails, pictures, and texts from a couple of our undercover field officers with the same guy's name or image of him, his record label, and the whole entourage!" Said agent Hernandez as he pointed at the computer screen. The computer had pictures of Antonio, Brainhead, and his squad in the VIP pics of Antonio and twin leaving the club. Pics in the parking lot of Antonio and twin in a blue Lambo. Pictures of some more black men with the same type of t-shirts as Antonio. R.I.C.O Ent. Pictures of the same guys jumping a young man and putting him in the trunk of a white Malibu.

"Wait a minute. Where are the agents who took all these photos and witnessed the assault and kidnapping.? Asked homicide detective Sosa.

"We're in the process of locating them now!" Said, agent Hernandez.

They stopped at the part when the young men in the white Malibu were picking up the rapper Brainhead.

"So, all these rap guys are involved in some drug click or something?" Said, detective Sosa.

"Yep, according to our sources, the twin left club LIV with Antonio Deangelo and ended up in a hotel room riddled with gunshots and a smoking gun in her hand along with her twin and another young man. They all were strapped! Where is Mr. Deangelo? How did he survive this shooting and what part did he play in all this!?" Asked Hernandez.

"We have an APB out on Mr. Deangelo as we speak." Said the female agent named Maria. Also, I found out the charm or emblem worn by the male victim is a medallion worn by the rapper Jon-Jon and his entourage!" Said the female agent. "I've had some agents and officers dispatched to the club LIV to question the rapper Jon-Jon and his entourage!" Said the female agent.

"Good job Maria!" said Hernandez. Just as he was about to walk off, he was approached by some more FBI agents.

"Hernandez, it doesn't look good!" Said, agent Patrick Lowery.

He just came on the scene, so Hernandez is thinking agent Lowery is referring to this crime scene.

"No shit! 3 dead Lowery!" Said Hernandez.

"No, No! I'm not talking about this scene. I'm talking about another crime scene you know with 2 undercovers we had on the rap label guy and his click!" Said Lowery.

"Yeah, where are they? Said Hernandez.

"Probably being digested by some alligators out in the swampy area of the Everglades. Their undercover car was located off Highway 41 towards the swamp. Then a young black male was found dead from bullet wounds and he was wearing a R.I.C.O Ent. T-shirt. The only thing that was found of the agents was a tennis shoe with foot and ankle still inside and a decapitated head with a big tooth mark in his chin!" Said Lowery.

Agent Hernandez stood there in shock.

"And oh...the head...the guy had dreads," Said agent Lowery. "We found a lot of spent shell casings, so a shoot-out took place in the swamps!"

Hernandez was putting it all together. The agents were following the white Malibu after they picked up the rapper guy. So their surveillance led to the swamps! "Put an APB out on the rapper guy they picked up from the club!"

"Yes sir!" Said the female agent as she immediately started talking into her Walkie-talkie.

"Man, what the fuck!" Said Brainhead.

Awakening me from a nod I was catching on the couch.

"Wha, what wassup?" I said reaching for my strap.

"Look, man!" Said Brainhead as the reporter was talking on the news.

"A triple homicide at the Vagabond Hotel on Biscayne Boulevard led authorities in search of a rap label owner-CEO Antonio Deangelo for questioning. Mr. Deangelo was seen leaving club LIV with one of the female victims and also was seen leaving excuse me, was also seen going in the Vagabond Hotel with the female victim and was later seen on camera leaving the hotel with two men who were arrested in the parking lot of the hotel. Chaotic driving was taking place of people leaving the hotel. The two men were in possession of semi-automatic and automatic guns. Also, developments at another crime scene in Miami. Miami homicide detectives and the FBI found the remains and body parts of 2 missing FBI agents who were working undercover at club LIV investigating rap label owner Antonio Deangelo and crew. A body of a young man wearing a R.I.C.O entertainment T-shirt which is Mr. Deangelo's record label. The undercover agents were on surveillance when they went off the radar they were following some R.I.C.O Entertainment affiliates when a known rapper was seen getting into the car that the agents were trailing. Authorities are looking for the rapper Brainhead who is signed to Antonio Deangelo's R.I.C.O Entertainment for questioning."

"Maan, you see this shit!!?" Said Brainhead. "The fucking feds was following us all time!"

"Maan, fuck" I said as I stood up pacing back and forth my mind running like a mufucka.

"Bru...what we gonna do?" Asked Brainhead. "

"I'm thinking about calling my lawyer and get him down here to turn myself in."

"Shit, fuck that shit I ain't turning myself in." Said Brainhead.

"Naw my nigga you lay low. My situation is beatable. They ain't got shit on me especially if the two young wolves don't open their mouths about nothing else! Shit, they were my security. They saw that I was in danger and didn't have any other choice but to blast."

"Shit my nigga, I don't know about that!" Said Brainhead. "Remember they said FBI, so you know they bout to come with the bullshit offering deals and all kinds of shit."

Brainhead was right! If this is a federal investigation anyway, they ain't going to let a nigga go unless we beat the
charges.

"Fuck naw! You right Brainhead! We both gotta lay low.
We got to get the fuck out of the country!" I said.

Chapter 29

"You'll never get away with this you fucking immundo una rata!" Said Conswela and spit in Carlos Desendez's face.

Carlos reacted by slapping Conswela to the ground. It wasn't much she could do, because he had her handcuffed. He reached down and tore away Conswela's shirt and wiped the spit off his face. Then he threw the shirt down on top of her.

"I'm going to draw your nigger boyfriend to me or you'll just tell me where he stays and you and your aunts make it out of this alive.!" Said Carlos. Carlos and a couple of his henchmen had kidnapped Conswela, two of her aunts, and a first cousin. He knew it would be hard to get to Renaldo or Anita, but Conswela would be a little easier. He knew how she frequented upscale clubs and like his son, she was hard-headed. Meaning after strict warnings about being out without security was a no-no! He found out where she lived first through one of his young henchmen. He had met her on a dating site. Within no time, the young handsome henchman had charmed Conswela. So, on their 1st date, Carlos had trailed the henchman to her house in Dallas. Now that he knew where she stayed, he came up with a plan to draw his enemies to him.

His young henchman and Conswela had planned a date

on the particular day of the kidnapping. When he showed up at her house she was in for a surprise.

"Hey mami, you look great!" Said the young henchman as he greeted Conswela at the door with a hug and a kiss as she exited her house."

"Hey Papi, thanks!" Said Conswela as they got into the Tahoe. When he closed the passenger door his chivalry turned into ultimate betrayal, because one of Carlos' henchmen was on the back seat ducked behind the passenger seat. In his hand was a rag soaked in some type of chemical and he swiftly put the rag to her nose and mouth. She bucked for a couple of seconds, but she wasn't strong enough to fight her abductor off. Nor could she fight the chemical that knocked her unconscious within 10 to 15 seconds. Carlos was on the third-row seats.

"Who else is in the house? Asked Carlos.

"I think she said 2 of her aunts and a female cousin." Said the henchmen.

"Go back to the door and ring the bell and we will kidnap them too!" Said Carlos.

When the henchmen went back to the door and rang the bell one of the aunts opened the door immediately.

"Ah, what did she forget?" Said the aunt.

"This is for you!" Said the young henchman who took out a pistol and made his way in the house with Carlos right behind with a drawn pistol.

""Aaaahh, what's going on?" Screamed Conswela's aunts and cousin.

"You know who I am" Growled Carlos as he pointed the

pistol in Garcia Abregado's old auntie's face. Once he said that she frowned, squinted her eyes, and recognized Carlos.

"You fuckin una rata bastardo!(You fuckin rat bastard!" Has hecho lo suficiente para mi familia! You have done enough to my family!"

"Fuck you and your family!" Said Carlos as he hit the 78-year-old Mexican lady with a pistol knocking her out. "Cuff them like the law!" Said Carlos as he put the cuffs on the elderly woman.

They took all of them to the truck and drove away. Now, in the Mexican desert with all the women laying on the ground face down being recorded on an iPhone. Carlos had snatched Conswela up and was questioning her as two of Carlos' henchmen stood over her two aunts and female cousin who was about 27 years old. They stood over the women with axes in their hands and black ski masks on. All the women including Conswela were crying and whimpering. Carlos was holding the phone recording the events which were about to take place.

"Ahora voy a hacer una pregunta este tiempo solo si respondes estas preguntas de la manera equivocada una parte del cuerpo de tu gente forma parte!" Quien fue responsable del asesindo de Carlos Desendez Jr.""Now, I'm only going to ask these questions one time and one time only. If you answer these questions the wrong way , off comes a body part of your people!"" Who is responsible for the murder of Carlos Desendez Jr?"

Conswela was sobbing harder now. "I don't know!"

Carlos looked at Conswela intently as to detect a lie or the truth! He held his gaze for 30 seconds looking into Conswela's eyes.

"I promise Carlos, I don't know!"

He gave her a look of sincere sympathy and understanding as if he believed her and would show her some mercy, but Carlos' sudden shift in his demeanor revealed evil intent! With an evil grin, Carlos looked at his henchmen and pointed.

"Off with her left foot!"

"Nooooo!" Screamed Conswela as the young henchman raised his ax over his head and swung down hard at the elderly lady's left leg just above the ankle. The ax landed with a sickly sound/thud as it smashed through flesh, bone, and achilles tendons!

"Aaargh!" Screamed the elderly lady. In agony and pain, the older lady thrashed her head back and forth on the desert ground.

"Te pudiera en el infierno inmundo una rata!" "You'll rot in hell you filthy rat!" Screamed Garcia's older aunt.

"Yea, not before you!" Laughed Carlos.

"Please...I don't know!" Screamed Conswela.

"What's the nigger number, Anita's number, and your nephew's number? Asked Carlos as he held her the phone. She was hesitating.

"Right foot," Said Carlos.

"Wait! Okay, okay!" Cried Conswela as she struggled with the phone. She finally unlocked it.

Carlos strolled through the contacts until he found Anita's number and Renaldo's number. He didn't know Antonio's name. "What's the nigger name?" The one who I saw in the car with you that night you eluded me at the hotel.

"I don't know! I have lots of black friends!" Said Conswela.

"Right leg" Interrupted Carlos.

"No, no, no!" Screamed Conswela as the young henchman raised the ax again bringing it down on the elderly auntie's leg cutting it off right at the knee.

"Aaargh!!"

Screamed the old lady as she writhed and shook. She was almost dying from shock. If her heart didn't give out on her first.!

"His name is Antonio!" Screamed Conswela.

Carlos was planning on sending them group videos and photos just like they did him when they killed his son. He went straight to Antonio's number. Marked Anita, Antonio, and Renaldo and sent them the video message!

Carlos was planning on sending them group videos and photos just like they did him when they killed his son. He went straight to Antonio's number. Marked Anita, Antonio, and Renaldo and sent them the video message!

Dallas, Texas

Anita was at home in her mansion at West-lake in Dallas, Texas relaxing after a long day at her office. She was thinking about all the drama that had been going on within the organization during the past year. The drama with Carlos Desendez and now the new developments with Antonio down in Miami. She knew that the feds were involved according to what she had seen on the news. She didn't know whether to cut all ties with Antonio now that all the violence is drawing heat.

Sure, she and her people didn't have anything to do with

the violence that had happened recently down in Miami. She knew if the feds were involved already that it's a possibility that she and Renaldo could be under investigation...again!

As she was laying back thinking, her phone vibrated on her nightstand. She picked it up and saw it was a video message from Conswela's number. So now she's wondering what kind of video is coming from Conswela. Once the video was downloaded, it was a total surprise to Anita!

"Oh dios mio!" ("Oh my god!") Said Anita as she looked at the screen. Two old women laying on the ground with their hands tied behind their backs whimpering! One was in total agony bleeding and her right leg had been cut off in two places and bleeding very freely. Two men with ski masks stood behind them with axes in their hands. A young woman laid on the ground. Then it registered in Anita's mind and she recognized the old woman and the younger woman. These were Garcia's aunts and niece!! Somebody had kidnapped them and Conswela. She couldn't see Conswela, but she heard her in the background.

"Please Carlos, Don't do us like this.!" Said Conswela.

"Carlos!" whispered Anita. Just as she said it Carlos started slapping Conswela to the ground.

"Shut up, bitch!" Said Carlos. "Now you all know how it feels to see a loved one get slaughtered!" "Think about it, the universal laws of reaping what you sow!" Carlos signaled with his hands to one of the masked men.

"Off with her head!" Said Carlos. With that command, you heard screams and cries as the masked man played executioner and brought the ax down on the older woman's neck decapitating her.

"Aaah!" Screamed Anita along with the women in the video.

"Immundo una rata!!"("Oh, you filthy rat") screamed Anita through tears.

Carlos turned the phone to him. "Gracioso tu amenaza fue contra productiv!" "Funny, your threat backfired huh?" The threat the nigga sent me after killing my son! A family member a day or something of that sort for me not coming to court. Guess what? Fuck court I want blood!" Said Carlos into the camera on the phone.

"Off with her head.!" The second ski-masked executioner swiftly brought down his ax into the second old Mexican woman's head at the ear lobe. He hit the ear lobe on purpose making it a messy situation because it was making the beheading difficult. The goon had to place his right foot on the old lady's back to gain leverage in wrestling the ax blade from the woman's head and jaw! Screams of agony came from the woman and a lot of... "What the fuck!?"

"Turk and CaiCO's Island!" I said as I watched Carlos Desendez video message.

"Bruuu" you live a very interesting life my nigga! Never a dull moment!" Said Brainhead as he was shaking his head in disgust but, smiling as he turned away from the video.

"Hell naw man!" Laughed Brainhead.

"Dem folks for real!" Said Lansky

"Maan, what the fuck!? Who is dem folks man?" Said Brainhead as he paced the floor of the condo.

"Long story, but he mufuckin enemy!" I told him. "This snitching ass Mexican playing some dirty games! He sat on the stand on my plug's old man in a big conspiracy case back in the days and he helped get him a life sentence! He was a government star witness and a top underboss in my potna's cartel. So, you know he gave them the business and told everything and got a downward departure (rule 5.k1) In his sentencing he escaped from the witness protection program and been trying to get some get back in his son's murder. He thinks I had something to do with it as well as my plug."

Brainhead and crew was kind of looking at me in awe.

"This nigga knocking mufuckas off for the cartel!" Said Brainhead. When he was locked up I always used to say, my big homeboy, classmate, pop is a mufucka!"

We all started laughing at my lil bro as I gave him some dap.

"You already know (hcn) high caliber nigga!" I said.

"High caliber nigga!" Said Brainhead. Well, whatever my nigga we all in, fuck it."

I then put my focus back on the gruesome video message to see Conswela laying on the ground crying and speaking incoherently in Spanish. That tore at my heart even though me and Conswela was only cut friend, friends with benefits, etc... I still had a love for her as a person and as my partner Garcia's youngest sister.

"I hope Antonio is looking at this! Said Carlos into the phone as he walked over to Conswela and put the phone close to her face. "Say goodbye to your nigga friend!" Said Carlos.

As Conswela wept as she looked into the camera. "Goodbye, Antonio! I know you're going to get this rat bastard!"

That's when all of a sudden the phone raised up as if Carlos was passing the phone to someone else and he did. Now, Carlos had the ax.

"Come out and war! Come out and find me!" Said Carlos

as he raised the ax above his head and brought it down hard chopping Conswela's head off. "Come out and find me!" Said Carlos and put the phone down facing Conswela's lifeless yet pleading eyes.

Chapter 30

Everybody was sitting around quiet. Renaldo sat with his mother consoling her as she spoke unintelligible Spanish between sobs into her son's shoulders. Me, Brainhead, Lansky, and Dingo just sat there quietly ready to put in work.

Nonetheless, after I watched that disturbing video message that Carlos sent all of us in a group text. I called my private pilot and got him to fly back down to Turk and Caicos Island to scoop us up and fly us to Dallas. I got to see about my plug and their family! They're the reason I'm a multimillionaire and my loyalty to them is immeasurable. I had already call Chi-Chi to see how things were looking in Atlanta and they weren't looking good!

"Man, the feds are everywhere!" Said Chi-Chi.

"Like where?" I asked.

"Bru everywhere!" Said Chi-Chi. First, they hit yo main office snatching computers, ledgers and oh they took your secretary in! They went to you're record label office confiscating shit! At the same time, they were at your real estate office. Oh, they got to your old lady Tanya."

"Nooo!" I responded.

189

"Yea my nigga!" Said Chi-Chi.

"Maan, fuck!" I said.

"Man, that ain't all they done hit our business looking through records, computers, and ledgers not to mention the IRS is rolling with them!"

"Man, this is some bullshit!" I said as I got up and lit a cigarette.

"When I got the call I didn't go that way! Um ducted off and bru they raided the fucking warehouses, the logistics spot, and that white boy Paul is shaking like a dog shittin cinnamon seeds!" Said Chi-Chi.

"I haven't been there at none of the spots lately to supervise or oversee daily operations, so I wasn't."

Had a shipment come in and stored there at the warehouse or had some left out by transactions to other suppliers & distributors. By now I was getting so much work that there was never a drought and so much money! Cash that I had apartments and houses that I used the bedrooms to just store money! Throwing it in there by the luggage and duffel bags like Frank Matthews in the early '70s! After having that conversation with Chi-Chi, I was partially shook, but I won't bend or break so I got back in tune with the matter at hand.

"Where can I find his folks!?" I asked.

"His immediate family, all of them are in witness protection!" said Renaldo.

My wheels are turning in my head like a slot machine. I want to get to Carlos's bitch ass so bad, but we don't know where to find him. We heard he was back on his feet down in Mexico, but that would be almost suicide unless somebody who knows the lay of the land and is trustworthy kind of lead us to him.

"What's up Renaldo? I know you got some soldiers here and down there.

"What you wanna do? You got to keep them wolves eatin!" I said.

Renaldo looked at me with contempt in his eyes as if I was challenging his gansta which I was.

Even though he burst his gun that night at the condos. His base of operations is in Oaxaca, Mexico where he lay his head...

"I don't know, but that's where he operates!" Said Renaldo answering the challenge.

Brooklyn, New York
10:30 AM

John-John and Big Lo were chilling at one of Big Lo's spots discussing what to do.

"So, wassup? You think Antonio knows that we was trying to knock him off? Asked Jon-Jon.

"Look, young nigga after all that carnage them niggas left behind. Hell yeah, he knows and you can bet somebody out yo crew got tortured probably. Then that nigga done put 2 and 2 together when they smoked them twins and the other nigga in the hotel!" Said, Big Lo.

"Not necessarily, it could've been a robbery gone bad for all he knows!" Said Jon-Jon.

"Bru...I know you're sharp! I know you seen the news and that internet shit! The report of one of your crew members being kidnapped outside of the Vagabond by some niggaz.

The same hotel where 3 people out of your crew just got smoked when they went back to club LIV to pick up that dumb and stupid nigga Brainhead... I know how they get down and they now know you're the enemy. Jon-Jon, out of this ordeal I'm the only one in the clear!" Said Big Lo proudly. At least that's what he thought.

Man, the feds looking for them niggaz though. Heavy too, Jon-Jon had acknowledged this information before the media put it out there. The police, Miami homicide, and the feds pulled up on him at club LIV during his album release party. Asking him questions like did he know the victims in the hotel and their relation to him. They wanted to know did he know anything about the guy being kidnapped in the hotel parking lot. So, he knew the feds were looking for Antonio and Brainhead, but actually, the shit had gotten deeper than anybody knew...except the feds.

11:45 AM

Columbia, South Carolina

Front Office

"Now, misses George where did you first meet Mr. Antonio Deangelo?" Asked special agent Bruce Livingston from the Organized Crime Investigation Unit of the Southeastern District.

"On Facebook," answered Kadia. The feds had followed and stopped Kadia the day she went to Atlanta to Antonio's office questioning Antonio about the disappearance of her cousin Brad and his cousin. It didn't take much effort on the feds part to turn Kadia into a rat because she already had that in mind!

"I think he was in prison at the time. You know how they have cell phones in prison. So, we kept in touch through Facebook then he got out we exchanged numbers and went from there."

"When did the drugs come into the picture!" Asked agent Bruce Livingston.

"I don't remember, but maybe 6 or 7 months after he had been out. He started asking questions about whether I knew anybody that was hustling and I told him about my cousin Brad hustling crack."

"Ms. George, is this the cousin who has since come up missing?" asked agent Livingston.

"Yea, yea that's the one. Him and his cousin and it's all my fault!" cried Kadia. "If I wouldn't have never hooked him up with Antonio he still would be living!"

Agent Livingston and another agent exchanged looks which meant press the gas. The other agent winked his eye at agent Livingston and went into bad cop mode.

"Listen Kadia, you need to tell any and every other thing you know because I don't think you're keeping it real with us. You did more than just hook them up.

You played the middle woman and the mule. Yes, you went to Atlanta more than once and trafficked drugs for your cousin and boyfriend."

"He ain't my boyfriend!" interrupted Kadia.

"You moved cocaine and heroin up and down interstate 95 for Antonio's R.I.C.O organization!" Screamed agent Bad Cop as he jumped out of his seat. "On conspiracy to possess, supply and distribute cocaine & heroin those are your charges!"

"I only did it a couple of times!" Screamed Kadia out of frustration for incriminating herself at the same time.

"It doesn't matter, you're still facing a minimum of 10 years for one count of conspiracy!"

"10 years? I ain't fucking did nothing!" Said Kadia.

"Maam, you just admitted to conspiracy to supplying and trafficking drugs!" Said the special agent.

He went and grabbed a law book off of a desk. It was a title 21 U.S.C.A. federal law book. He turned to the pages that showed sentencing and punishment. Key 3225 statutory section requiring the imposition of a mandatory sentence of life imprisonment for those persons convicted of engaging and continuing criminal enterprise. (CCE) who are principal administrators, organizers of leaders of schemes that involve...

"Hell naw, shit I wasn't involved in no organization!" Screamed Kadia.

"If you say you've moved drugs for Antonio one or more times darling you were playing the role of administrator because you oversaw....

"What do you want?" Said Kadia interrupting the bad cop.

"What we want is you to tell the truth about everything you know!" The few times you have moved for Antonio and his dealings with your cousin. Testify about what you told us and we'll make sure you get a rule 5k1 in your situation.!"

"What's that!" Asked Kadia.

As if on cue the good cop, special agent Livingston produced a form along with federal rules of court. The law book was turned to the section that displayed the rule 5K1.

As Kadia read it she thought of her missing cousins and the guilt she felt for introducing the two and she thought of her children. "Fuck, Antonio!" Said Kadia through tears as the good cop passed her some Kleenex and a pen.

Baton Rouge, Louisiana
(12:35 PM) Location: Federal Building

"So...., you're telling me that you and Dee Bradford a star NFL receiver got some type of athlete involved point-shaving ring or something?" Asked federal agent Homer Atwater.

"Well, yes and no." Answered Raquin. James Raquin was a 3-year starter for the Saints and a friend of Dee Bradford. Dee played for the Seahawks and he was a star receiver. The two go all the way back from little league to college football. They both played at Grambling, one as a receiver and the other as a defensive back.

They're both clients at Deangelo's sports agency. Antonio, basically let Dee's mother recruit him to his sports agency as he was fucking her a lot. Antonio started meeting with her shortly after she recruited her son. He had to fuck her because she had a body that wouldn't quit. She liked Antonio so much that she helped or was an accessory to violating NCAA ethical rules and laws. Antonio gave Dee a 2018 BMW M6 Convertible hardtop and through his mother, he had also given him a Camaro. Then he flew him to Atlanta and let him get VIP treatment at his strip club.

Furthermore, he chauffeured them around and put them in a couple of videos with Antonio and the crew. Of course, he had the mother super straight financially like the R. Kelly song "Step in the name of love". Like he did it for love was how Antonio was playing the situation, but all the time his focus was on the son. To convince him to sign with his sports company. Pull some strings to get him drafted no later than the third round with millions added onto sure money with endorsements.

Dee brought his friend Raquin James in to sign with Deangelo Sports Agency and Antonio worked hard to negotiate good deals for both of them. Enter the Underground which was the shady side of the sports world that was known for bookies, point-shaving, and Vegas. At first, none of that was even on Antonio's radar until his partner Jamey who ran his "slick pick ticket racket" out of his sports bar mentioned it in general.

Them Antonio thought about ex-bookies and mobsters that he did time within the federal penitentiary. All the cases he had studied in the law library and some of those were about sports gambling. A light bulb went off in his head and he thought about his white partner that he went to school and played football with was out in Vegas.

His partner Chauncey used to work in a casino and had ties to them and the bookies. Antonio flew out to Vegas and met with Chauncey, some bookies, and some mob dudes. The rest was history and all Antonio had to do now was turn some of his athletes into point shavers, etc. At that moment Antonio only had 2 athletes that were football players. Now Dee had a little street in him, but his partner Raquin had a lot of street in him or so it seemed at that time. Antonio was a good judge of character and had keen instincts. So, he knew Raquin had some sheisty-shit in him, but greed took over and Antonio put him up on a task.

After their rookie season, Antonio started cutting into both of them about the art of point shaving. Antonio had already built a good relationship with them to the point that they would listen to him not just out of respect but what he stood for which were loyalty, love, respect, and getting lots of money. Not to mention they liked his style because he vibed and kicked it with them as if he were their age.

When the time or moment arrived, both of them were starters and had great seasons. They performed well in the playoffs and for all their great performances and statistics in games, there was also a clause in their contracts for bonuses, etc. However, Antonio was also given under-the-table bonuses like duffel bags stuffed with money just like back in the '80s and '90s. When the dope boys would pay some high school football players for their performances. For example, a $100 bill for every tackle, interception, or touchdown. Now, it was used for buttering them up. The game had escalated, and Antonio was on some mob shit.

He explained to them that they had an impact on the way a game turned out. Being impact players, especially Dee, he asked them did they know anything about Vegas gambling that spread worldwide. Sports gambling that was somehow connected to Vegas and Antonio explained all they didn't know like point spreads, over and under, and if it's controlled a little or a lot. A lot of big money exchanged hands in favor of the winner. Antonio laid it on smoothly as to how a player is conscious of this and becomes part of the scheme. Behind the scenes, he could reap a handsome harvest under the table after every game.

"Bru, I don't know. It sounds like I'll be selling my soul. That's mob-connected ain't it?" Said Dee.

"Fuck, the mob. You must don't know who you down

with!" Said Antonio. "I got this, they'll only be dealing with me and my people and I'll deal with y'all. If anything, any kind of threat I catch wind of I'll deal with it in a swift manner. They get eliminated asap ya dig?" Said Antonio.

The 2 football players were still slow to give an answer to the indecent proposal.

"I'll tell you what, whenever ya'll make up your mind up let me know what you think." Said Antonio.

"What I'll get? Asked Raquin.

Antonio broke it down to him. "You're a lockdown cornerback. Passes that you can normally break up let them go in certain situations that is."

"Situations like what?" Asked Dee now highly interested.

"Say the point spread on the game is 6 or 7. Seattle, you all are favored to win without the points ya'll are giving them away. Antonio went in-depth explaining and they got the picture on what to do and how and what their payments would be for shaving points or throwing a game. After their second season, they were recruiting some more NFL players, NBA players, and a couple of college football players. One of Raquin's little cousins had got caught up in some dope cases and couldn't stand the pressure and flipped on Raquin. Raquin was telling who the real boss in the whole scheme.

"You're fucking agent?" Asked the federal agent Atwater.

"Yes, my agent just like I told you. He came to us in the beginning with the idea and he paid us in cash and sometimes gifts."

"Such as!" Asked agent Atwater.

"Big homes, some we never stay in or we might give them

to family members, or we would sell them! Most of the homes were owned by my agent's real estate company."

"This got agent Atwater's attention for sure now. He would love to get the IRS involved in tax evasion and forfeiture case against a sleazy agent. If Raquin is telling the truth. He didn't have anything to do with drugs you and your crew was selling.

"Naw!" Answered Raquin.

"I told you his name is."

"Hold it!" interrupted agent Atwater. "We'll get to that in a minute." "Let's get back to your agent. "Are you willing to testify in trial or before a grand jury to what you told me so far?

"Yeah!" Said Raquin thinking about the disgrace he would put himself through by ratting and he's thinking about his career and family.

"Okay, what's your agent's name and the name of his agency?

"The name of the agency is Deangelo's Sports Management and my agent's name is Antonio Deangelo!"

Agent Atwater immediately googled the sports company. "The owner and CEO of this agency looks familiar."

"He's a record label owner also!" Said Raquin.

The detective googled Antonio and read about him. He put him in their database and was astounded by what he was reading.

"Damn, this guy is already a wanted man. He's some kind of drug kingpin. Been to prison for murder and federal drug charges and they're looking for him in connection with murder and drugs." With that information, agent Atwater got on the phone and called the FBI office in Atlanta, GA. "This motherfucker's a big fish!" Said agent Atwater in his Louisiana twang.

Chapter 31

"You're one lucky muthafucker, Abregado!" Said one of the correctional officers. Referring to the latest developments in Garcia's appeal of his form 2255 federal habeas corpus. He had finally prevailed and received a new trial in his case. He was being led to the receiving and departure area in the prison to be flown back to Texas for a new trial.

"I wouldn't call it luck!" Said Garcia. "It's a blessing! I was dealt a great injustice by the U.S. government!"

"Ha, ha!" Laughed at the C.Os. "Great injustice? You're a top-notch cartel leader! They got you just right. I don't see how in the hell you got a new trial!"

Garcia just smiled at the comment. He knew his attorney would work things out. He also knew that he could depend on his faithful and loyal friend Antonio to keep the government's main witness Carlos Desendez from showing up to the trial. He had heard about all the chaos Antonio was facing. He had made a vow to himself to stand with Antonio. Through the madness and help him with all his might and power. Also, he had made a vow himself to avenge the deaths of his baby sister Conswela, his niece, and his aunts.

During the government's appeal which was really a time delaying tactic. Besides the issues, they had already raised against Garcia. They inserted facts from their star witness on the run from the witness protection program and asked that the courts at least put the retrial on hold until they captured Carlos.

Also, they made claims of witness tampering stating that Garcia had Carlos' son murdered. In an attempt at intimidation and he had hitmen looking for Carlos at that present moment. To no avail, that issue was lost, because it was without merit or proof. True, when Jr was murdered there was the voice of a black man issuing a warning telling him not to show back up in court. But it wasn't enough because there was no evidence it was from Garcia, just an assumption.

"You all have a nice life!" Said Garcia to the CO in the receiving and departure area.

"You'll be back!" Said one of the CO's as Garcia was led to the waiting airplane.

Oaxaca, Mexico

"When is this bitch going to surface?" I whispered to Renaldo.

"I don't know!" Said Renaldo.

We were laying in wait close but at a safe distance from one of Carlos' spots. We had been in Oaxaco, Mexico for a week now looking for Carlos. At first, it seemed as if we were on a witch hunt but thank god for the power of the almighty dollar. Renaldo had some of his people infiltrate Carlos' new organization and learned some valuable information. Carlos had this spot where he would meet with a few of his men and local drug dealers. They would play poker into the wee hours of the morning. We weren't sure if Carlos was actually in the poker house, but from the info, we had received he goes to the house every night. A black Suburban pulls up and the driver and passenger get out. Both of them are armed with assault rifles and the driver walks towards the rear of the truck and the passenger walks towards the front of the truck. They're both doing a recon of the area around the side of the house and looking across the street at the other houses.

Luckily, Renaldo had already found out who owned the house directly across the street and bought it. He quickly and quietly moved the family to a better house miles away and paid them handsomely.

We were at that house watching. After the driver and passenger made sure the coast was clear. The back doors of the Suburban flew open and out stepped Carlos Desendez with 2 more men assumed to be his bodyguards.

"Fucking piece of shit." Said Renaldo as he was looking through a pair of binoculars.

"What, that's him ain't it?" I asked. Reynaldo passed me the binoculars. I looked through them and affirmed my curiosity. "Yea, that's him!" I said.

"Wasup?" Said Brainhead as he was grabbing his AR15.

Renaldo held up his hand. "Wait, let's try to figure out his movements. We have to be careful on his turf."

"Shit, how long that gon take? Said Brainhead.

"I don't know, we just have to wait until the time is right!" Said Renaldo.

"Man weight broke the wagon!" Said Dingo using an Alabama saying. "I was getting antsy myself. I don't know Renaldo we can't be bullshittin."

"I know it's dangerous down here, but we got to get it while the getting is good!" I know, I know but we can't slip right here! Our lives depend on it!" Said Renaldo.

We all looked at each other. "Right, Renaldo we agree but we got to strike soon. If we have to wait him out and put a tail on him. Find where he stays or just run-up in that bitch over there across the street or try to sniper his ass off over here.' I Said.

Everybody was quiet as the wheels were turning in our heads on what to do. Nobody wants to be on any suicide type of time, but I wanted to get this muthefucka just as bad as Renaldo for what he did to those women. I went ahead and sat down and relax because I had been pacing like hell? We sat there for hours and hours and no movement across the street except the people that was coming to gamble.

"Damn, that many people fuck with this rat? Said Brainhead referring to the people who were going to his gambling spot.

"Unfortunately, people tend to forget, or they just don't give a fuck." Said Renaldo.

As we sat there sweating the gambling house, I was thinking to myself.

Here I am, a fucking mogul, a big-time black entrepreneur that owned a hot record label known publicly and had almost celebrity status by default. An ex-con that came up from nothing when I got out with nothing but balls and my word. Now, I'm back knee-deep in the game and rich as a fuck.

Yet, I'm facing some charges and maybe going back to a unites states federal penitentiary or the grave. Loyalty is not just a word it's a way of life. In the words of big-meech and oh so true.

"Yo, he's coming out!" Said Renaldo.

Snatching me out of my thoughts. I jumped up and grabbed my AK. I peeped out of the blinds and just as he said. Carlos was heading down the steps with one bodyguard in front and one behind him. I almost took a shot out of the window.

Renaldo got on his phone and called some of his people who were already riding around the area.

" Estas cerca condominio?(Are you close to the condominium?")

"Yes," Says Renaldo's people.

"Be on the lookout for a black Suburban!" Said Renaldo. "Trail her from a safe distance and keep me informed on their movements. We'll catch up with you! Let's go." Said Renaldo.

Renaldo had a driver outside in a white old Excursion in the backyard. We went out the back door and piled in with our artillery and eased off in the direction of the black Suburban.

-

Chapter 32

FEDERAL INVESTIGATIVE BUILDING

The feds had Paul Fredricks under intense questioning concerning Deangelo Transportation-Logistics and Warehousing and the 400 kilos of cocaine and 100 kilos of heroin they found in a secret package stored in the warehouse Paul was running.

"Um telling you! I don't know anything about any drugs!"

"Bullshit" Said DEA agent Thornton. "We've done a background check on you buddy! You did time with Antonio Deangelo and he recruited you to run that business for him because you have a degree in logistics!"

"So, what does that mean?" Said, Paul.

"It means that you had full knowledge of the whole operation and what comes in and out of that warehouse. Plus this syringe we found in your arm when we busted in on you and the dope we got out of your hand when you were damn near wigging out and nodding. It is the same product we got out of the warehouse. High quality and all!" Said DEA agent Thornton.

Antonio already knew of Paul's drug use from doing time with him. He used to sell Paul synthetic marijuana and heroin in the joint. He knew Paul had a degree in logistics like the DEA agent said so he truly recruited Paul! So to speak Paul didn't know he was being recruited. Antonio had locked it in his mind and added Paul to his vision. As a top prospect in his scheme of things.

Once they both were out and Antonio came up. He went and found Paul in Birmingham, Alabama, and gave him a job. Once he realized Paul was still an addict, but a functioning addict though. He kept Paul straight with the girl and boy(cocaine and heroin).

"Explain that smart ass!" Explain the ounce of cocaine and the ounce of heroin we found at your condo." Said DEA agent Thornton.

This surprised Paul because he didn't know that they would get a search warrant for his place after he was arrested. That information brought Paul all out of his stupor.

Now, federal agent Johnson of the Georgia FBI office was about to pour it on nice and thick. "Son, you've already been in prison for 2 felonies. One for vehicular homicide and the other was for federal bank fraud. Paul, these are all federal charges you're facing."

"How's 2 ounces federal?" Said, Paul.

"Because this is a conspiracy investigation. An ongoing R.I.C.O investigation and continuing criminal enterprise investigation. Son, the felonies you already have will enhance your points to your base offense level which enhances your sentence. If found guilty."

"No, no, nooo! How am I in conspiracy with anything that I do?"

"Son, your actions and the role you played in furtherance of the conspiracy to distribute and traffic..."

"You keep saying conspiracy, I didn't know anything about drugs coming in on these trucks till one day Antonio and his partner Chi-Chi was there looking through pallets of turkey in the freezer. That's the only time I swear!" Squealed Paul.

The room full of feds and the DEA agent who was on the other side of the dark windows gave each other high fives as the DEA agent and federal agent Johnson looked at each other. That's when agent Johnson like magic produced a motion for a rule 5k1 downward departure form/snitch form.

DEA agent Thornton pulled out the syringe and the same pack of heroin that he pulled from Paul's hand during the raid and sat it on the table between them and Paul.

Paul was salivating at the mouth like a rabid dog. He had a mean monkey on his back and he was damn near going through withdrawals.

"Paul, you want a cigarette?" Asked federal agent Johnson as he produced a pen and sat it on the form. He gave Paul a cigarette and a light.

Paul was thinking about his freedom and he was hurting like hell.

"Are you going to give me that?" Asked Paul as he damn near grabbed the syringe and dope.

"Not until you talk." Said DEA agent Thornton as Paul snatched the syringe and dope.

"Let me get a shot first I'm sick." Said, Paul.

"Fuck you!" Said DEA agent Thornton as he jumped up as if he was about to leave.

"Okay, okay, okay" Screamed Paul as he took off his glasses, rubbed his eyes, and shook his head. He took a hard pull off the cigarette and once he was through blowing the smoke out he opened his eyes and took a deep breath.

"Okay, where do I start." Said, Paul.

Meanwhile
2 Floor up
Federal Building

"Maam, we can charge you with conspiracy to money Laundering so far!"

Said Federal agent Bill McCarthy.

"Oh yeah, how are you gonna do that? Said Tanya whose Antonio's girlfriend and business partner in their real estate company.

"Simple, you were helping your boyfriend Mr. Antonio Deangelo clean up drug proceeds by laundering it through the real-estate company and you had knowledge that it was drug money."

Tanya wasn't fazed by the questioning at all. She knew that they didn't have any evidence on her with anything. She had been through questioning with the feds years ago in the early 90s when she was dealing with her ex-husband. Plus, she and Antonio went through this before and if anything happened. They were careful how they talked on the phone so she knew they didn't have any recordings or records that incriminated them.

All of their paperwork was legit. The only thing she was worried about was if they picked the lawyer chic up would she hold up.

Birmingham, Alabama
Federal Headquarters

"Ms. Janice Riddlesburg, am I pronouncing that right?" Asked federal agent John Vickers from the Birmingham FBI office.

"Yes, attorney Janice Riddlesburg and I demand to know what's going on." Said Janice.

"Maam, that's what I want to ask you." Answered Federal agent Vickers. The feds had been doing their homework on Antonio and swiftly connected Attorney Janice Riddlesburg to Antonio's real-estate company and she was the trustee of some land trusts and he was the beneficiary. In a land trust, the beneficiary owns the trust and the trust owns the property. In a land trust, nobody knows you're the beneficiary except for you and the trustee.

The only way they will find out is through a court order. So, when the feds got their search warrants for Antonio's businesses. The warrants allowed the seizure of all computers and records. Once, they ran the trust agreements they got a hard-on. Trust agreements in real estate stay with the beneficiary & trustee and it discloses the beneficial interest. Numerous holdings got their attention like an overseas property named Aniyavest, GA. An apartment complex in the Virgin Islands, timeshares, 300 condos, and a full-fledged spa resort.

The feds and the IRS were saying that the offshore corporation Aniyavest, GA was used by Antonio Deangelo to channel drug money through the apartment complex and resort spa. They're making claims that money was laundered by making off-the-books and under-the-table transactions with the sub-contractors involved in the construction of the apartment complex and resort spa.

With their line of questioning Janice knew that they didn't have anything on her. They just saw her name on record as the main attorney for Deangelo's real-estate company.

"I see that you're on a witch hunt. I have nothing to say and I want to see my lawyer."

"Ms. Riddlesburg, you're a lawyer so I'm sure you understand the type of investigation you're caught up in. All I need is your cooperation to grant you immunity."

"Am I under arrest?" Interrupted Janice.

"Ms. Riddlesburg, I repeat that this is a federal investigation on some R.I.C.O charges." Said the agent slowly. "Against the owner and operator of Deangelo Enterprises. Your clients which implicate you by default."

"I have nothing to say give me my phone call." Said Janice calmly.

Agent Vickers made a bridge out of his fingers and placed them on the table then shook his head stood up and went to get a phone.

Chapter 33

WEST TOWN

D'Anthony, Antonio's son was ducked off in his baby mansion in the West Town. He left Alabama as soon as he heard the feds were looking for his father and crew. His step-father relayed the message through a throwaway flip phone as soon as the investigation got heavy.

Once he found that his name wasn't implicated in anything he got the fuck on. Got out of dodge before his name was implicated in anything. They already knew the ties he had with his father both legal & illegal could easily put him in the mix of an investigation. He was very cautious in his dealings with Antonio on the illegal side. He heard about his pops when he was growing up through his mother and some of the people in her family but when he met him he knew he was the real Mccoy.

Once he went around him and witnessed the kind of work he was moving he had to stay sharp. He fell right into the groove because he had it in his blood. Plus, he was already hustling good on his own. Pops just gave him that boost that he needed. What every young dope nigga dreams of. A fireplug

212

that don't mind putting that work on you and dealt fairly across the board with quality work and product.

D'Anthony had a plugin Chicago where he grew up with his grandfather and family, but it wasn't like Antonio's work and organization. Pops dope was fire like Chi-town's dope and he had a lot of it. He would give him a price just a few thousand above the price he was paying for a key of heroin and cocaine. So, it was a must that he was fucking with Antonio full-time. At first, he had that young nigga attitude towards his pops.

"I'll jack my plug, he ain't been in my life anyway. I don't know him as a father" but he quickly dismissed that thought. His pops was making up by making him rich. Had him where he was strong in Alabama and he had a crew of his childhood friends in the Chi-town eating like pac-man which in turn had him eating like a king. At the same time that made him some enemies up there. Like his old plug slash mentor and o.g.

So, now he had his own problems that he would handle accordingly. First, he had to make sure his name wasn't on any federal indictments. He grabbed his phone and texted his stepfather on one of his throwaways. "Name ain't on nothing?" After about 3 minutes his phone vibrated as a call was coming through, but it stopped immediately then a text came in shortly from the same number.

"No, but lay low will find out more."

D'Anthony's vice narcotics stepdad got back to him and D'Anthony was confident he wasn't on any indictments with his father because he was real smart. He didn't do business recklessly. In fact, he took more precautions than the average young man. After meeting and chilling with Antonio a couple of times clubbing and doing a little business. They planned an exclusive way of doing business.

A suggestion that D'Anthony made that he would be dealing head up with pops instead of the middleman. That's how a lot of people ended up in a conspiracy investigation. If the middleman is under investigation or he got popped and started cooperating with the feds. Plus, he talked Antonio into getting a phone and that they were the only ones who kicked it on that phone

In codes only.

Antonia liked that idea because he operated in that manner anyway. The only thing was if his office was bugged whenever he went there he didn't talk illegal business at those meetings. He may talk about rap groups in Birmingham, Alabama, but that was it.

When D'Anthony left Alabama, he took the remainder of work and stash money with him. The only thing left was dope that was already in circulation. Once his two main lieutenants get that money and sent it to him. He wasn't going to be fucking with Alabama for a while. If it caused a drought fuck it, because if the feds missed him in their current investigation. He wasn't going to give them a second chance especially in Alabama.

Interrupting his thoughts was a computerized buzz through surround sound in his house that was letting him know that someone was buzzing at the gate. Which was the gun line in D'Anthony's mind, so he immediately grabbed the AR-15 and looked at the monitors which were connected to the cameras surrounding his property. Even though only a few people knew where he laid his head when he was in Chi he still took precautions. He smiled at the face which was looking up at the camera.

"Sharita!" Said D'Anthony. Sharita was a pretty reddish-brown Dominican chic. A face and body like Tahiry, Joe Budden's ex-girlfriend. Sitting behind the steering wheel of a snow-white Bentley GT Coupe that would make the average nigga smile and do a quick appraisal of this woman.

"Are you gonna let me in D'Anthony or are you gonna just stand there and stare me down through the camera?" Said Sharita knowing she got him pegged just right. He hit the open button without a word for Sharita. Sharita was about 2 or 3 years older than D'Anthony so she was just finishing college and was pursuing her career as a journalist.

She was interning with various magazines, but her dream was to own her own magazine. D'anthony helped her all the way through college financially. When she graduated, he got her the all-white Bentley GT Coupe and he got an all-black Bentley. She knew what he was doing and she didn't agree with it especially when he got his own record label.

When she pulled up he greeted her at the door.

"What's up mami?"

"Wassup papi!" Said Sharita as they engaged in an intimate kiss. "Wassup with all the mushy shit?" Joked Sharita as they entered the house. "You glad to see me and do you miss me papi?

"Of course!" Said D'Anthony as he turned her around and kissed her some more. He loved Sharita like crazy. She proved her loyalty when she stuck by him when he went to juvie two times. Once for possession of crack and the second for shooting somebody in a gang-related incident. She was his heart and he was hers. She just wanted him out the streets. D'Anthony didn't waste any time showing Sharita how much he missed her by undressing her and making love to her all day. After they got through they went to sleep for 3 or 4 hours.

His throwaway kept buzzing so it woke him up. It was a call and text from his stepfather.

"Talked to some friends in high places! Pops wanted for questioning about some missing drug dealers in South Carolina and some R.I.C.O investigation. More specifics later!"

"K" D'Anthony texted his stepfather. The only thing on his mind now was how deep was the R.I.C.O investigation and how it would affect him. He looked at his sleeping beauty and thought that if he's missed in this investigation he would chill and get out of the game.

-

Chapter 34

HOUSTON, TEXAS

FEDERAL BUILDING

Since Garcia was back in Texas in federal lockup his family was visiting him except Renaldo. Anita had filled her husband in about everything that was happening. She would communicate with him using codes in case the place was bugged so that they wouldn't know what they were talking about.

"They changed the new trial date again!" Said Garcia

"You can imagine why." Said Anita.

They both understood the reason was that the government was trying their best to locate Carlos Desendez to no avail because they couldn't find him. They guessed that he was south of the border in Mexico without their government's help and they still couldn't locate him.

The Mexican government was dragging its feet about finding Carlos. They had a few Federales that were trying to locate Mr. Desendez. Then, it seemed as if they could care less about a snitch. You could tell some of them were being paid off.

After 2 weeks of stalling, Garcia's attorney put in a motion for the court to dismiss the case. The court didn't rule on it, so he sat on the motion and had the decision in limbo. Garcia, actually wasn't nervous about the situation, because the key witness against him wasn't going to show up. Plus the other witnesses either recanted their stories and testimonies or were missing. He just laid back and continued being patient because he knew that Carlos would be murdered soon by his son and Antonio. Since he made a declaration of war there's no showing up in court.

Oaxaco, Mexico

We had been cold trailing Carlos and his goons for the last 30 minutes until he went to the countryside to a ranch that was off 2 main roadways. Took a right off the highway and a left off the countryside highway and another deep left onto a long-ass dirt road. I was sure in my mind that we were being led into an ambush. But, to my surprise, it wasn't we parked on the main road and walked down the dirt road. There were 9 of us in all. Fucking rap label owner and one of his rappers that's famous are going to battle helping some cartel people.

"I'm sure there are cameras everywhere!" Said Renaldo.

"We've got to flush them out!" Said one of Renaldo's shooters who spoke English."

"You're right!" Answered Renaldo.

Before any cameras could pick us up we spread out and slowly inched our way closer to the front of the house. Then, out of nowhere.

"Bwaaaa!" There was a shot and you could tell from the sound of the report that it was a big ass gun. Someone was hit and I didn't know who it was. All I knew was how to pull the trigger on my rifle and aimed it into the darkness because I believed it was some sniper shit. One of Renaldo's men had a grenade launcher and he busted that mufucka dead at the house through a front window causing a nice explosion.

"Kaboom!" A third of the front of the house was smoking in flames followed by six or seven different assault rifle bullets. Somebody was down and two of the Mexicans had grenade launchers. We were being met with great resistance to the point that we had to spread out wide and were close to being put in retreat mode.

But, thanks to the grenade launchers they were slowed down. We knew a few of them in the house were down because we heard screams of agony. The sniper was taken care of because I got him when I blasted off in the dark to our left. We knew there were at least 3 or 4 of them left unless there were some already at the house like the sniper in the dark.

Renaldo gave his grenade men the signal to blast off. "Kaboom!" Within seconds after Renaldo's command, his amigos were yanking triggers back-to-back. "Kaboom, Kaboom!"

"Aaii!" Came a scream from the burning house. We crept to the burning house slowly. Taking cover behind a couple of jeeps and the black Suburban. Taking advantage of the smoke.

"Plow, plow, plow, plow!" shots echoed from the house and sprayed the Suburban. Nobody was hit and the return fire was reimbursed with quickness. As we approached the house, we noticed 2 men quickly retreating out the back door. All of us shot at them but we were too slow because they escaped and disappeared into the darkness. We really didn't have time to look for Carlos Desendez, but we still took a chance looking at the 5 bodies scattered around the house. To our disappointment none of them was Carlos.

"That was him who escaped," I said.

"You're right!" Said Renaldo as we exited the house.

"Let's check on Francisco, he got hit. Said one of Renaldo's men.

I knew somebody got hit and I was glad it wasn't me or mine. We got back to the body on the road. Renaldo and his men stood over him shaking their heads and making the sign of the crucifix over their chests.

"Let's go!" Said Renaldo as we all trotted back to the truck we came in. All of us were quiet as we rode out thinking to ourselves

"How the fuck I get so deep in the game!" At the same time we're probably thinking the same thought I was having the most and that was this snake slithered away again!"

Federal Courthouse

Atlanta, GA

Press Conference

"We are here today to announce that the U.S. government has a sealed 32 count indictment for residents of the city of Atlanta, GA and abroad. A few arrests have been made here in the city of Atlanta as well as Columbus, Savannah, and West Point Georgia!" Said the U.S. Attorney General for the Georgia region.

He had pictures flashing on a big computer screen as he held his conference.

"We have arrests to be made in other states including our neighbors in Louisiana. More arrests are expected to be made in other states connected to the said indictment."

"Mr. Redding!" No disrespect but you haven't told us

what these indictments and arrests are for." Asked a reporter as everyone kind of laughed.

"Oh, I'm sorry I got carried away. This is a widespread R.I.C.O indictment among other things." The government didn't want to put it all out there to the press, because that may put other possible suspects on notice. Besides, they haven't caught up with the main players in this drug ring.

A week after

Raid in Mexico

That night in Mexico after missing Carlos we made our way back to the safehouse. The next morning, we made our way back to Dallas, Texas. I learned the feds had a R.I.C.O indictment for me along with some more shit. They didn't have anything on Anita and Renaldo which was good, because Garcia was about to get out through the court system. Good news for my partner and bad news for me! Like Bunbe said, "One day you're here and the next day you're gone." Looks like when he comes out, I'll be going in. Fuck that, whatever was about to happen they were going to have to catch me. That was my frame of mind at this point and I was wondering where the R.I.C.O charges came in.

Before they get me, I've got scores to settle before or if they get me. I have got to catch up with this bitch Jon-Jon. I felt like he played me and I needed to get to a couple of my stash houses to get my money.

We parted ways with Anita and Renaldo then made our way to Atlanta. I couldn't go home because the feds have been there. I couldn't go to my mother's or any family member's house. So, I went to one of my fire duck offs out in Dunwoody, GA.

Brainhead couldn't go to any of his or his family member's houses. So, he went to his girl's crib where her mother also stayed who didn't like Brainhead period. He knew that she didn't like him but didn't think she disliked him to the extent that she would call the police but that's what she did.

After an argument that took place between her, Brainhead, and her daughter. It was normal for Brainhead and his girl's mother to get into an argument. Her mother was always getting into their business over petty stuff and she would go off by telling him that this was her daughter's house.

He would say "Who do you think pays these bills.? Who buys the groceries in this bitch? Who cush you're smoking, etc.."

So, they were going back and forth about some cereal or something and the mother went right on and called the police while Brainhead was talking shit to his girlfriend. Something was telling him to leave so he grabbed his car keys and left. While he was driving he ran up on this dude named Andrew who fucks with his girl's sister. He pulled over and picked Andrew up and drove around telling him what just happened.

While he was talking to Andrew, he noticed Andrew was on the phone.

"Who you talking to?" Asked Brainhead stopping the story he was telling. When Andrew stuttered for a minute and told him he was talking to his girl's sister. Brainhead quickly figured out that Andrew was telling them where they were.

"Fuck nigga, you was telling them where I was." Before Andrew could answer Brainhead was beating him in the head with a chrome .45 and didn't stop even when the police came. They almost had to shoot him to stop him from hitting Andrew and that's how Brainhead was captured.

Mandingo was captured when he was trying to sneak and holler at his kids and baby mama in the Bowen Homes. Lansky was captured and killed when he was in a shootout against some dudes who they made turn something in. They had caught him by himself on East Boulevard down past Grady's Memorial Hospital in the middle of traffic.

Lansky had left his car in traffic and was running in broad daylight with an AR-15 assault rifle shooting at his rivals. When the police pulled up he let off a volley of shots at them too. Unsuccessful in his getaway Lansky held court in the streets and shot it out with the police like on TV. He ended two of their lives and they ended his.

With that taking place and finding out that he was wanted by the feds for a R.I.C.O indictment that made them intensify their search for Mr. Brainhead, Chi-Chi, Sonny, and Lamont. I found out my son ducked the indictment and I made sure I checked on my young wolves that were locked up in Miami because they saved my life. At first, they were speaking on a bond then they took it away, so I figured the feds had a hold on them.

I got with some chics and gave them a hundred and fifty thousand in cash money apiece and directed them to hire the best attorneys in Miami to rep my lil partners. If they haven't snitched that is and I'll find that out when the lawyers sign up to rep them. I've found out the feds raided my numbers spots, sports bar, bookies, writers, and so on.

With their raids, they're taking houses, property, money,

and cars. They're running up on a lot of my money that I hadn't collected or had a lot of people sitting on. They're running up on pallets of dope at my warehousing-logistics spots. Posing with that shit when they got Paul at my main warehouse hub for distributing and supplying. I heard they got 100 keys of heroin and 200 keys of cocaine.

My warehouse in Hurtsboro, Alabama they confiscated $20 million dollars in cash which they found in big cans of baked beans plus 150 kilos of cocaine. Pictures on the news and newspapers of money and cocaine. Also, they ran up on a couple of 100-pound bales of marijuana. Anywhere my name was on a business as the owner the feds raided. They even went to my cousin's modeling agency because my name was on the paperwork as a co-owner and out of that raid they came up with some of my money. A lot of it. Remember, my cousin Bam-Bam in Jacksonville was collecting a lot of my weed money which in turn comes from my distribution/supply operation running out of Holatee Trail which distributes anywhere from 20-30,000 lbs. weekly.

So, if I don't go get it but once a month minus what she's getting paid and funnel it through her business. She's sitting on 40-$320,000 in that range. They didn't go to her salon and nail spots because my name wasn't on it. Yet they arrested her for conspiracy to aid and abet a R.I.C.O organization.

They hit my sports agency and arrested my agents. The feds even arrested some of my star clients who were ratting on me and some of my athletes. Even the college boys are being implicated with the exception of my plug. Everybody who was doing direct business with me or for me legally was being arrested and squeezed.

As for the dope side, they were rounding muthafuckas up left and right. In Atlanta, Virginia, The Carolinas, all kinds of places. I found out what got the folks on my trail. The violence which escalated in the city was what put the icing on the cake., but some niggaz caught them late-night cases. What we haven't heard about had started working with the folks who in turn was dealing with people under my lieutenants. All this stuff had started happening around the same time. Some dudes out of Pensacola, FL got busted with a lot of synthetic marijuana and agreed to start working for the government.

We don't even deal in that fake shit, but he told the feds that not only would he get his synthetic plug. He knows some high rollers over in Georgia he would get. He told them about the high rollers, the plug on his coke and loud were members of a drug gang called R.I.C.O the record label, guys.

The feds made some calls and found out we were on the fed's radar already. When he came to shop with the people under my lieutenants he was wired up and his phone was tapped. So, when he did that it started a ripple effect. He had been working a couple of months and all those buys were adding up. He wanted something bigger than what his plug could sell him. That's when his plug called my lieutenant and my lieutenant called me. Now there's surveillance on a lot of phones with Kadia's help.

Now, the feds got her to set up who was husting for her cousin Brad. When they got him he folded and started telling the feds about how Brad and his cousin are missing. He told how I paid him and that he was buying and getting fronted cocaine, heroin, and weed by me. I learned of all this through

Anita and she learned all of this through their inside source in the FBI.

With everything that was going on Anita still had my back. She knew that I was smart enough to not lead the people to her. I text my mother through a throwaway phone I gave her a while back. This phone was for times like now. I told her that I loved her and gave her addresses to spots that I had duffel bags and suitcases full of money. I went to some of my main spots and got a lot of money.

I had a few safety deposit boxes in alias names in which I went and got some money, fake passports, credit & debit cards. Packed a few clothing items and placed them in the undercover Taurus and me and one of my side chics pulled out.

They had let my girl Tanya out on an ankle bracelet. They didn't have anything on her for real. I text her on one of us in case of emergency throwaways. She let me know that she was okay and how they froze our accounts, but she would make it. I told her about a spot I had in Alabama in a place called Beauregard outside of Opelika. I told her where the money was located and that she could have it if she split it with my daughter.

The last time I counted that money it was a little over 10 million dollars and there was some loud, weed and cocaine there. I told her to leave the work and we'll figure out what to do with that later. After I handled that I had a score to settle and that was with Big-Lo and Jon-Jon.

-

Chapter 35

After their meeting in New York Jon-Jon and Big Lo separated. Big Lo headed back south to Atlanta. Jon-Jon kept doing shows with no care in the world. Besides, his new album had just dropped, and he had to promote his album by traveling around on tour.

Even though he hadn't heard of Antonio being captured by the feds. He felt like Antonio wasn't crazy enough to try and make a move on him because he found out that Jon-Jon was working with Big Lo to have him erased.

He heard about Brainhead's arrest and said out loud.

"Damn, why couldn't I get him before the feds did?" Oh well, he thought to himself. He felt bad about the twins and Kabo. They rolled with him from day one. Nonetheless, he still had an entourage out of Texas with him watching his back in every city and every state that he toured. He felt as if he was being watched and that someone in the crowd was down with Antonio and his R.I.C.O organization. He knew how far Antonio's words went and how deep they were. They didn't get everybody.

Stone Mountain, GA
11:45 AM

A semi-drought was going on and a few renegades still put work out on a smaller scale with lower quality and bigger prices. Big Lo out of New York was doing the most. He pretty much had the streets on lockdown and had the game in a chokehold.

He felt like he was in the clear from any of the bullshit that was going on. How wrong he was and he was soon to find out. Big Lo's specialty was tricking off with some strippers just like his late nephew Faygo.

Antonio had snuck around and got to his Haitian partner who was from Opa-Locka, North Miami. He put his fine Haitian cousin on the lick with one of her fine Jamaican partners. For the money Antonio was paying they would've set Jesus up. They caught him on one of those magic city Mondays by double-teaming him with lap dances while dropping Molly's in his drink at the same time.

One made a suggestion of leaving the club with him and the other was telling him how good they would fuck and suck him and that did it. The fool took them to his mansion in Stone Mountain to do some freaking and have a menage et trois.

While they were freaking Big Lo in the jacuzzi, Antonio was already in the house with them. Before they went to the jacuzzi Lo didn't know the Haitian girl was already hipping her cousin to the layout of the house and that the cousin was hipping Antonio.

Antonio brought one of his nephews because he knew how to disable alarms and perform break-ins. His nephew went by the name of Yung Shoota! He was game to do dirt with his uncle. Antonio never put him into the game, because he felt he wasn't ready. Instead, he let him in the studio but didn't ever give him the push he needed because he was so busy. His nephew was trigger happy so he was down for work like this.

Anyway, Antonio waited good until they had Big Lo in ecstasy in the jacuzzi before he popped up on them. All of a sudden, all freaking stopped and the strippers jumped out the jacuzzi pronto. They headed out and wiped down everything they had touched.

Big Lo was surprised. "What the fuck?" Said Big Lo when the girls left him naked in the jacuzzi staring down a .44 Bulldog revolver in Antonio's hand and a .38 Special in Yung Shoota's hand.

"What do you want from me Antonio, you into robbing now?" Let me get to my safe and I will give you everything in it. It's about $7.5 million and you can have it all just let me live.

Antonio was there to kill him but what the hell he might as well get the money and split it with his nephew who in turn had a smile on his face thinking about the money.

"Let's go get it!" Said Antonio throwing Big Lo a towel and his robe. They followed behind Big Lo as he walked up the stairs to the bedroom where the safe was located. He loaded all the money in a big duffel bag and gave it to Antonio.

"Here man, I understand the feds are after you and you're probably kind of despe...."

"Boom!" echoed the .44 Bulldog Antonio was holding as he interrupted Big Lo by shooting him in his knee.

"Aaargh, I thought you were gonna let me live? Screamed Big Lo as he writhed in pain holding his knee.

"Bitch ass nigga you didn't want me to live, you or Jon-Jon!" Said Antonio and with that being said Big Lo knew he wasn't going to live because he had been found out.

"Man, ma- man I don't know what you talking about B!" Screamed Big Lo looking like the dude on 4 brothers. The one Victor Sweet made eat the french fries off the floor.

This time Yung Shoota shot him in the shoulder causing him to turn over. Antonio looked at his nephew and nodded giving him the green light.

"Hold up, Antonio!" Screamed Lo but it was too late young Shoota was putting 5 bullets into his head.

Chapter 36

Garcia Abregado was about to go back in front of a federal judge to get a reversal and remand for a new trial. He was prepared mentally for whatever.

"All rise!" Said the bailiff as the judge came out of his chambers and took his place on the bench. He went through a few documents for effect.

"You all may be seated! What I have before me now is case number 97-04762 appeal number Sd-737-048 in the southern district of Texas. In the case of the United States government vs Garcia Abregado, I see that this has been an ongoing appeal on your behalf Mr. Abregado and you have been successful in winning a new trial. I also see that the defense has put in a motion for the case to be dismissed."

"That's true, your honor!" Said Garcia's attorney.

The government's attorney was whipped and you could see it on his face. He wanted to say something but his written objection had already been denied and he no longer had a star witness or any witnesses for that matter. The few witnesses that were left recanted their testimonies.

"I see, I've already denied the government's objection and therefore I see no use in still holding this man. The defendant's motion to dismiss case number 97-047-62 is granted. Court is adjourned, you are free to leave Mr. Abregado." Said the judge as he banged his gavel.

Just like that Garcia Abregado got his life sentence reversed by the judge so he walked out of the courtroom into the arms of his wife Anita who was in tears as a free man.

I was hot on Jon-Jon's trail and I didn't know if he was aware of Big Lo's demise. Whether he was or wasn't he was about to meet his demise. I was aware of Jon-Jon's whereabouts by following his tour dates.

Also, I had put a couple of gangstas on his trail. Right now, he was in Tennessee not far from me. I had some childhood friends that had relocated to Tennessee that was getting work from me exclusively without the middleman, so they were clear of the indictment.

Plus, there were some stone-cold killers that were located in Nashville that followed Jon-Jon to Memphis. Once I arrived in Memphis, I checked into a low-budget hotel. Well, my side piece did, and I laid low. My partners were at the venue where Jon-Jon held his concert just chilling and waiting.

Jon-Jon's Concert

"Sippin on some sizzurp, sip, sip, sippin on some, sippin on some sizzurp."

"Ya'll ready to pour up in this mutherfucka!" hollered Jon-

Jon as three-six mafia and U.G.K.'s classic boomed out of the speakers.

"Guess who I got wit me in this bitch? Screamed Jon-Jon as the Three-Six Mafia walked on the stage. The crowd went wild for their hometown heroes. All of them had baby bottles full of drank, a purple syrup.

"Um trill working the wheel a pimp not a simp. Keep the dope fiends higher than a Goodyear blimp!" Jon-Jon was rapping pimp c's part of the song.

He had already been smoking cush, popping mollies and now he was drinking promethazine. He was good and high so he didn't know if he was just being paranoid when he noticed two cat-eyed niggaz backstage staring him down. The younger of the two was bobbing his head and the older one wasn't.

My two homeys were brothers and they had eyes like a tiger or bobcat. The oldest one named Trent was brown-skinned and the younger one Terry was a reddish-orange nigga with almost sandy hair and a big cut on his left jaw. They looked menacing and up to no good to Jon-Jon.

My partner Trent worked at the center so it was easy to keep backstage passes.

Jon-Jon looked back towards the audience to kind of play his spookiness off. Was he definitely spooked or was it the drugs?

"Naw!" He thought to himself because of the line of work he was in he knew when he was in possible danger. In the crowd, he spotted two dread head niggaz bobbin their heads and one of them was making trigger signs with his fingers.

"Fuck!" Thought Jon-Jon to himself as he hurried through a verse and looked backstage at the spot where he'd seen the two cat-eyed brothers and they were gone. Quickly, Jon-Jon eased offstage and searched backstage frantically for his team.

Little did he know but all of his entourage were outside in a van. Trent got six big dudes that he knew and two of them were white. To go backstage with some fake FBI badges, bulletproof vests, and jackets with FBI emblems on them in bright yellow to confront Jon-Jon's whole entourage without any resistance. They quietly led them out back to a van then handcuffed and shackled them.

As Jon-Jon was searching for his crew, he ran into this light-skinned policeman. Well, at least that's what he was supposed to be.

"Yo, Jon-Jon wusup bro!"

"Hey, man wusup bro!? Answered Jon-Jon. "I'm looking for my entourage and security."

"Damn bro, I believe the feds got them!" Answered the cop.

"The feds?" Screamed Jon-Jon.

"Yea!" They took them outback. Look bro I'm a big fan of yours and I don't want to see you get locked up."

"Locked up, I ain't did shit! Said Jon-Jon.

"Look, follow me and I'll cover for you. I'll sneak you out of the other exit which leads to the front." Said the cop as he crossed the lobby and opened a door that led to a long hallway

"What about my tour bus?"

"Fuck your tour bus right now homey. Follow me."

Jon-Jon was hesitant for a second but thought like fuck it the police and my fan was helping me getaway. He ran down the hall with the policeman/fan and took a sharp left and there was a bright shiny red exit sign. Showing the way out and the cop ran through first. He motioned for Jon-Jon to hold up for a second, then he looked left and right to check if the coast was clear. Then he looked right and nodded his head like the coast was clear but really, it wasn't. At least not for what Jon-Jon was thinking and he found that out quickly.

When he exited the door a black bag was placed over Jon-Jon's head and he was kneed in the nuts at the same time making him fall to the asphalt. His hands were quickly cuffed and he was thrown into the back seat of a soccer mom's van.

Once Trent and his brother pulled off the fake officer walked back inside the building as if nothing happened.

My partners hit me up in a text. "Mission Complete!"

I hit back and told them where I was and 20 minutes later they were pulling up in a regular van. I had already had my side piece chic get another room at a better hotel and got her to drop me off. Not without removing my loot, I left her a little something in a small cosmetic bag I left on purpose. It was about $30 thousand dollars because after I handled my business with Jon-Jon I'm going on the lam(on the run).

I got in the van with Trent, his brother, and a knocked-out Jon-Jon.

"Y'all got a spot!" I asked

"Yea!" Said Trent and pulled off. After riding for 20 or more minutes we ended up in a rural area called Munford. Wasting no time I snatched the punk-ass nigga by his ankles and yanked him out of the van. He bumped his head against the tailgate and that woke him up.

"God damn, man!" Said Jon-Jon.

I snatched the bag off of Jon-Jon's head and when he

gained focus and realized it was me. His eyes started blinking rapidly like he couldn't believe his eyes.

"Yes, it's me nigga!" I said as I pulled out the .44 Bulldog.

"Hold up, boss man! What's the deal? Where is all the plex coming from? Um yo best artist nigga!"

"Bitch ass nigga you the deal!" I said and kicked him in the mouth. "You didn't think I was gone find out nigga?" "You are working for Big Lo to knock me off. That fat ass nigga dead if you didn't know and you done got rich off me!"

"Bru, I promise that I wasn't going through with it. I was going to hip you.."

"Boom, boom, boom!" barked my .44 Bulldog interrupting Jon-Jon. All 3 shots went to the head.

"Let's roll!" Said Trent and we hopped in the van and left Jon-Jon there to rot.

Chapter 37

"Famous rapper Jon-Jon was found dead in a rural area in Memphis, Tennessee. He was shot multiple times in the head. It seems as if trouble has been following the rapper.

A couple of weeks ago members of the rapper's entourage were found murdered in a hotel in Miami, Florida during his album release party. What's strange about that is the label that Jon-Jon was signed was R.I.C.O Records. Owner and CEO Antonio Deangelo was last seen at that hotel with a female victim of the entourage and was wanted for questioning but hasn't been seen since that night. Right now we have Captain Peloski of the FBI Tennessee Office. Hey, how are you, sir?"

"I'm doing fine, thank you."

"Captain, could you tell us what you have so far?"

"Well, this is an ongoing investigation so I'm not at liberty to divulge too much information. However, I will state that witnesses say the rapper left the stage after his verse on the song. He was seen backstage running with a police officer and was found dead later. Also, members of his entourage were found bound and gagged in a van in the back parking lot."

"But weren't these guys in the van placed under arrest by the feds?" Interrupted the reporter.

"Well, I have no further answers right now, could you excuse me." Said Captain Pelosi. He didn't want to let the public know that they had been infiltrated by some people posing as feds. To make matters worse his office was instructed by their superiors in the FBI to place some undercovers at the concert. Due to the severity of the investigation into a said record label, the undercovers were there but they missed the abduction of Jon-Jon. They thought it was part of the act because they totally missed the fake arrest of his entourage and a few local officers saw that part but were told by the white arresting federal officers that it was federal business and they're rounding up drug dealers so they got out of the way.

Captain Peloski was enraged because his superior was calling him and asking how in the world did this happen right under their noses. They flashed a drawing of the red police officer on the news.

"If anybody recognizes this face, call the secret hotline and let us know." Said the FBI spokesman.

In the Atlanta Office
Of the FBI

The feds had been working overtime trying to see whether the latest murder of the rapper Jon-Jon connected to the murders that took place in Miami, Florida of the famous rapper's entourage. They were working on leads from informants on the streets whose information was reliable in the past.

Reliable sources are what they're called and some of them gave information about the war that had escalated in the streets of Atlanta. Well, really killings of the enemies of the R.I.C.O organization.

They were told that before Jon-Jon was a rapper, he was

a hitman operating out of Houston, Texas with ties to some heavy drug dealing gangstas out of New York. Who in turn sub-contracted Jon-Jon's services to one of their O.G.s who stayed and operated out of Atlanta named Big Lo (aka Lorenzo Jenkins) who was found murdered recently in his mansion in Stone Mountain.

With all this information the feds discovered that Big Lo had a hit out on Antonio Deangelo and rap artist Brainhead for the murder of his nephew Fagin Jenkins aka Faygo.

"Let's get this straight, all of these murders may be connected through some rappers, business owners, and drug kingpins. A very wanted drug kingpin that we haven't captured yet?" Said special agent Dickinson.

"Right!" Said DEA agent Thornton.

"Well, we need to catch this guy and I mean like yesterday!" Said, agent Dickinson.

I was on the road like a runaway slave except I was riding with this fine-ass Puerto Rican chic my partner Trent hooked me up with. I'm halfway paranoid, especially when I saw the news. Since I've been in the limelight from my record label everybody and their mama knew how I look. Then I'm riding dirty as hell and I got 150 million dollars, 10 keys of heroin & 10 keys of cocaine on me heading to Detroit.

I got a partner from way back in the '90s that I met in the pen and he's there. I want to leave the country and head to my spots in the Virgin Islands but I know that's a no-no. I know that they have me red-flagged right now with a photo and all plus my property down there is traceable.

So, until things cool down I need to lay low up here and then I'll head west. My partner Garcia is out and I want to go see him but I don't want to draw heat to him. He texts me on the throwaway and I text him back to congratulate him. When I got to Detroit I had the chic get a room at the Cadillac Inn downtown. I was tired from the ride but I still blew a blunt of bud with the fine Puerto Rican because ain't no telling when I'll be able to fuck a woman again.

-

Chapter 38

D'Anthony had been laying low and fucking his girl for a week straight and she was glad that he was in the Chi permanent. They had been riding around in her white Bentley Coupe just checking out the scene. He had heard about Jon-Jon's murder and saw the news also. All he was thinking about was his pops. Antonio's son knew about the whole beef plus he knew when his pops Antonio found out that this nigga was an infiltrator, he was dead. Pops didn't play!

His stepfather informed him that he was ok but still to lay low for a while. As for his record label, he believed they had a freeze on it due to federal forfeiture laws. Which states that any business that falls within the scope of a federal investigation all operations are stopped when people start getting indicted. Any and all businesses under the controlling entity must stop running.

D'Anthony would have to work something out with Atlantic because he needed the power of a major distributor behind him. He had a couple of groups in Alabama assigned to him and they are blazing. They're hot and he needed to keep them hot. He had just started dealing with some old school friends who are rapping in the Chi and underground.

They were hot, so he has to get with Atlantic or find another distributor. As for the dope gang he's giving it up after he moves the work, he brought to Chicago which was 20 keys of heroin, 50 keys of cocaine, and 20 lbs. of loud. D'Anthony's stash was about 10.4 million dollars in cash, 6 million in the bank that he already transferred. Financially he was straight as he and his girlfriend rode through the Southside of Chicago. He'd seen a familiar face in a black drop-top 2017 Corvette at the red light.

"Stop the car!" Said D'Anthony. As they stopped his girl was letting the window down.

"What's up Tulu!" Said D'Anthony to the driver of the Vette.

"Aah fuck, wusup Tulu!" Screamed the driver of the Vette. The name Tulu was a private joke amongst the two about a crazy guy that they witnessed going berserk in a barbershop on some PCP or something when they were in middle school.

"You back in town fool?"

"Yea, to stay!"

"Hit me up, my number is...naw fuck that the light had started to change.

"Let's go to a restaurant to get something to eat."

"Follow us!" Said D'Anthony.

The driver of the Vette is a friend from his school days whose name is Sion. D'Anthony and Sion have always been cool even though they're from different hoods. He had to see what was up with Sion. Who knows maybe he's in the game and this may be a route that some of his work can travel through.

Since Garcia had been out, he had been laying low with his family. They rejoiced together about his freedom, but truly they were in heavy grief dealing with the deaths of Garcia's 3 sisters and niece. The brutal way that they had died was eating at him. For one, he felt like it was his fault because if he didn't put the hit on Carlos Jr. this never would've happened.

But, on the same hand, Garcia wouldn't be out either. It's like he sacrificed his family members for his freedom. With that thought, he sat and cried to himself. All he could think about was getting even with Carlos. Garcia had been in touch with Antonio and things had not been looking good for him. Garcia was very loyal to Antonio in exchange for Antonio's loyalty. Garcia was thinking about ways to help Antonio stay free or if he was captured get him freed.

Garcia was told by Antonio about his son that was raised in Chicago. Neither of them was aware of Antonio's son's status with the indictment. If he was clear and a standup guy like his father, Garcia had plans for him.

Detroit, Michigan

I had been in Detroit 2 days before finally linking up with my partner Brian. hadn't seen this nigga in years, since about the year 2000 at Talladega one of those federal joints. He knew my situation, so he agreed to come to my room.

"Wasup, nigga? Said Brian as I let him into the room.

"Wasup, bru? I said as I dapped Brian up.

"Maan, what the fuck you done got into?" Asked Brian.

"A bunch of bullshit!" I said.

"Bro, I have seen you all over the news and shit. You got to be careful on how you move."

"I'm hip!" I said.

"So, what's up? I know you got a plan."

"Yea...I probably have to lay up here for a minute 'til things cool off then I have to head for the border!"

"I feel you bru. So what's up? You need me to do something for ya?:" Wusup my nigga, I'm here!"

I like to hear people from back in the days talk like that and mean it.

"Actually, I do bru. I need a spot other than this motel. Somewhere laid back that's not too exclusive but not hood, you feel me?"

"I feel you my nigga. Maybe a house in a good neighborhood!" Said Brian.

"Exactly!"

Brian pulled out his phone and called somebody and within minutes had a house somebody wanted to rent to own and with five thousand dollars down would move me right in.

"Now, that's wusup. Now my second thing is I got some work that need moving." I said as I gauged Brian back in the days. Brian used to move work and rob people. A nigga that dressed almost preppy but gangsta. A person a nigga would misjudge, and he was a Y.B.I. affiliate which was a Detroit click from back in the days.

"Shit, bru I been running my own clothing store and I ain't been in the streets, but I know some niggas that do things." Said Brian.

I thought about what he said about his store.

"Okay, I'll get back at you on that but besides that, I'm cooling.

"Okay, I'll get with the dude in the morning on that house."

I went in my pocket and gave him a $10,000 scrilla roll. Then Antonio thought for a second went in his pocket and gave Brian another 10 band roll.

"That's 20 racks, 5 down on the house & 10 on some basic furniture and 5 for you to keep.!"

Brian's eyes lit up a little as he smiled. "You about your business, bru. I'll handle it all in the morning. Other than that are you good for right now?" Asked Brian.

"Yea, I'm Gucci! Just hit the phone in the morning. I may ride wit ya. You know, learn my way around."

"Okay, that's wusup." Said Brian as he walked out the door.

I hope this nigga still solid because right now I didn't need any bloopers. I had gotten the Puerto Rican chic to get two rooms to throw things off. After I fuck this Joseline look-alike from Atlanta love and hip-hop. I was going to break her off and send her on her way because I got work to do.

Chapter 39

The U.S. marshals had spread their net wide and long for the manhunt of CEO/Kingpin, Antonio Deangelo. All federal offices in the United States were on alert in the wake of the execution-style murder of the famous rapper Jon-Jon. The feds were in hot pursuit for the capture of Antonio. He couldn't be seen in too many public places because his face has been flashed on TV, electronic billboards on the interstate, and public freeways.

The media sensationalized the story prepping it for a movie. "So, it seems big-time CEO of famous rap label, entrepreneur and alleged drug kingpin wanted in a federal R.I.C.O indictment and a string of murders. Mr. Deangelo has alleged ties to a Mexican cartel whose boss has been released from federal prison through the court system."

On and on went the stories which later would earn Antonio Deangelo a spot on the front of a Don-Diva magazine as well as a spot in a United States penitentiary (U.S.P.). Possibly at a supermax like A.D.X. Florence, Colorado! The spot Garcia just came from. The place where Larry Hoover along with a lot of more high-profile gangsters. The feds had traced a lot of Antonio's family line so in those cities and states. The federal marshal had already hit and was still on the lookout. So far, the feds were unlucky, but technology brought them their break!

In big motels, they have their camera systems hooked up with the NCIC computer systems just for this type of situation to catch fugitives, wanted criminals, terrorists, etc...

The night Antonio stepped foot in that hotel in Detroit with the Hispanic chic the N.C.I.C. the computer went ape shit! As soon as Brian left the hotel that night, they apprehended Brian in the lobby and kicked both hotel room doors in while Antonio was fucking the Puerto Rican chic. At least he got a chance to get a nut.

"Hands where I can see them, loverboy." Screamed the feds once they were in the room with pistols and rifles aimed at him and the girl. Antonio didn't make any false moves; he just laid on top of the girl, hands outstretched where the law can see them. The way the police were killing blacks he wasn't about to make any false moves.

"Finally caught up with you Mr. Deangelo. You have the right to remain silent." The feds were reading Antonio his rights as they were handcuffing him butt naked.

"Let me put my clothes on man." Said Antonio. They handcuffed him and allowed him to put his clothes on.

"Bingo!" Hollered and agent as he opened Antonio's luggage and duffel bags and found the dope and money. They led Antonio out of the hotel and as soon as he hit the lobby he was met by cameras, news reporters, and paparazzi. Antonio didn't say a word, he just looked straight ahead as he was led to a black Grand Marquis with tinted windows and rode off to the federal detention center in Detroit.

-

Chapter 40

2 WEEKS LATER

ATLANTA FEDERAL HOLDING UNIT

The news of my arrest was plastered all over the news for 2 weeks straight. I was mad as fuck at first. I thought Brian had set me up, but then I found out that technology had got me. They were holding news conferences showing the drugs they confiscated in the investigation. They had shown the property, guns, and money as a whole and were posing with that shit.

They had the dope and money on long tables for display. They really tripped out about all the money and dope they got from me. A little under $150 million dollars in cash and 10 keys of heroin & 10 keys of cocaine.

"Mr. DeAngelo has ties to a Mexican cartel!" Said a prosecutor to the reporters.

"Which cartel?" Screamed a reporter. Questions were thrown around like crazy.

"Is he one of the next big drug kingpins like Frank Mathews from the '70s?

My first court appearance after the extradition proceedings was a fucking arraignment hearing.

The present Time

Damn, I guess you can say this shit is ironic, ironically stupid, or maybe even janky as fuck. That is to name this organization after one of the most feared law statutes the government can come up with to lock people up for a looong time. But nevertheless, it is what it is R.I.C.O (Real Individuals Caliber on High. That means a click of real niggaz but high caliber real niggaz. Big money getting niggaz. The majority of us are real street niggaz who love to get money but got enough sense to clean it up. Got sense enough to get educated to become entrepreneurs one way or the other with the same abbreviation as the government's United States code annotated title 18@1961 Chapter 96 Racketeer influenced and corrupt organizations.

The federal judge read the indictment and definition off as follows:

"Oh yeah, you heard it right, indictment! Racketeering activity means

1. Any act or threat involving murder, kidnapping, gambling, arson, robbery, bribery, extortion, dealing in obscene matter, dealing in a controlled substance or listed chemical which is chargeable under the state law and punishable by imprisonment for more than 1 year."

2. Any action which is indictable under any of the following provisions of title 18 U.S. c-201 Relating Bribery section 224 (Relating to sports bribery section 471 and 473 relating to counterfeiting.

"Damn, I know I don't fit all this shit that this cracka reading off!" Is what I'm saying to myself. And he continues...

"Pattern of racketeering activity requires at least 2 acts of racketeering on which on or after the effective date and the last which occurred within 10 years after the commission of a prior act of racketeering activity enterprise includes any individuals partnership corporation association or other legal entity.

"Do you understand this indictment which I'm reading to you, Mr. DeAngelo?" Said the federal Judge Barrett Thomas of the Northern District of Georgia."

"Yes, sir." I humbly answer when all the time I want to say fuck naw I don't understand, and he continues.

"The next indictment Mr. DeAngelo is under 18 U.S.C.A.2, 848 often referred to as the kingpin statute CCE (continuing a criminal enterprise). You are charged and indicted with 1 count of that. Now, I'm going back to the R.I.C.O charges and read the other counts that you're charged and indicted for.

I can't believe this shit is what I'm saying to myself.

"You and your organization are charged with 100 counts of racketeering activity as I explained to you earlier Mr. DeAngelo what constitutes racketeering activity and what is a pattern of racketeering activity. A pattern of racketeering activity requires at least 2 acts of racketeering. 10 counts of murder are linked to you and your R.I.C.O organization which took place on."

The judge is reading off these charges and indictments for murder and everything else they can pin on me and my click.

"17 counts of gambling in the form of running an illegal

gambling operation from and through Sports bars and gambling houses with illegal bookies taking in money for what they call slick picks which coincides with the bribery in sports in the form of point-shaving in college and professional sports."

A Couple of the athletes who are there to testify for the government shift uneasily in their seats as all eyes turn or cut their way. Shouldn't have fucked with them square bitch ass niggaz is what I'm saying to myself. Although, there were some real niggaz stand-up guys that were athletes that didn't flip on me so I got to be thankful a little about that.

"20 counts of sports bribery in college and professional sports mostly in the form of point shaving and 20 counts of extortion.

My lil young partner Brainhead is sitting there with a smirk on his face like fuck it while crossing his arms a little above forehead level in what they call the maxed out sign. He wasn't bullshitting, him and his goons with their T.S.I. (turning something in) thing. Extorting niggaz out of their work and money.

"Yea, I was living like young Jeezy say... (my goons got guns) tried to cool them young niggaz down and get them on the tip of drama only when necessary.

"5 counts of kidnapping" read the federal judge which was linked to a branch of this R.I.C.O organization called T.S.I.

I'm thinking to myself that all these niggaz who so-called extorted, kidnapped, or both were supposed to be gangstas and now they got a nigga in court about to testify on them.

"10 counts of bribery, 10 counts of dealing a controlled substance. All of these counts and charges are in direct correlation to your legal enterprise, entity, corporation Deangelo enterprises to the furtherance of conspiracy of your criminal enterprise.

"Mr. DeAngelo," Said the federal judge pausing and taking off his glasses for effect "In a 6 year period. You understand what's going on Mr. DeAngelo?" Asked the judge.

"No, not to this point," I answered wondering why do they ask all these dumb ass questions, I guess it's for the record.

"Well, I hope you will after this trial with the help of your legal team Mr. DeAngelo because you're in a lot of trouble." Said the judge.

I got lawyers on deck. Some of the best in the country so I'm not tripping. But now that we're up to date about a 6-year span let's see how it's going to play out.

-

Chapter 41

6 MONTHS LATER

My trial date is about to roll around and I had some fire-ass lawyers. One of them is Garcia's lawyer and they found out some of the government witnesses were muthafuckas my lieutenant's people were dealing with, not me. They can't establish any kind of relationships like seller or buyer. Nope. Supervisors like they worked for me. Nope.

Through electronic surveillance when they tapped my lieutenant's phone which led them to me, Paul the white guy who ran the logistics for me was rattin. Jamey who ran the slick picks was standing strong and my main partner Chee-Chee was working. Pressure from his ole lady made him turn himself in and give up all kinds of info.

I couldn't believe it, a couple of the football players were flipping on me about sports bribery. They came to me wanting me to flip on the Vegas bookies, my connects, the cartel, and my plugs. No way Jose is what they got from me. My lil wolves who were locked up in Florida stayed strong.

The broad Kadia was testifying along with a host of others. My girl Tanya was going to be straight along with my cousin Bam-Bam in Jacksonville. It was going to be a long trial with me and all the co-defendants. All I can do is sit back and wait.

Ever since Antonio's arrest, D'Anthony had been lying low. Him and his partner Sion had teamed up and had been putting heroin and cocaine into St. Louis and Gary, Indiana. However, he let Sion do all the footwork. He had family over there and knew a few people from when he was younger.

Sion had been getting money in Chicago on a smaller level, but D'Anthony introduced him to the weight game.

D'Anthony knew for sure that he was clear of his dad's indictments, but was still kind of taking it slow. He's still trying to get the record label back to pumping. It's just that the distributors knew his label's last name was R.I.C.O entertainment. So, that alone made the executives a little skeptical. He had potential with his label because a couple of his artists from Alabama were raw. Plus a couple of his artists in the Chi on his label were talented.

He had thought of changing the name of the label Antonio had been calling him every now and then to see what was going on in the streets. What was going on with him and the label etc? He told him that he would write a letter and sent it to his grandfather's house.

It wasn't long after their conversation that he received a letter from Antonio at his grandfather's house. It was a short letter but valuable.

"What's up D? I hope everything is going well with you. As for me, my future's looking dim, but you know I can handle it and I'm going to beat this at trial or on appeal. Anyway, I'll tell you later about the Benedict Arnold and turncoats. My trial is in another week you may or may not want to attend. If not, I understand and I don't blame you. My partner is interested in meeting you if you're still interested. He's a standup guy and if I haven't done anything for you this hook-up will make up for it. Just call him Migo when you text or call him. Tell him you're Antonio's son or just say this is D'Ant. Then he'll know who you are and wusup. I've already talked to him so stay up, stay focused, stay cautious and stay alive. One. Pops!!!"

P.S. keep a line of communication open for me and go see your grandma.

After D'Anthony got through reading the letter he was thinking like hell. He knew his pops was turning him on to the plug. Not just any plug but the cartel. He had promised his girl, mother, and grandfather that he was done but he wasn't so sure now. He had time to think about it though because since the federal sweep has been going on D'Anthony had stopped altogether.

He wasn't supplying his Birmingham, Alabama people which was his main plate nor was he supplying his Chicago people. That left things kind of dry especially if those customers and workers didn't know where to shop. He would make his mind up when he was close to getting rid of his leftover work. He really didn't want to keep moving dope through Chicago, because of the ill feelings it had caused with his old plug/ O.G.

He had to step to him and do like some players and talk it out before they get into some gangster shit and shoot it out.

Carlos Desendez had relocated to Tucson, Arizona ever since the failed attempt on his life at his ranch house in Mexico. He already knew who was responsible and he had lost 3 or 4 good soldiers in that attack.

He was now obsessed with the Abregados especially since

he learned that Garcia got out. True enough, Carlos knew he had violated by ratting on Garcia, but Garcia had done the despicable in his eyes. He had Carlos Jr. murdered for something that Carlos Sr had done. So, he got him back by killing Garcia's 3 sisters and a niece.

They struck back. Kool, thought Carlos to himself. All is fair in war and love. Carlos heard and saw the news that the nigger Antonio Deangelo was captured. He hated that because he wanted to kill Antonio. He still had his old phone from the witness protection and he was looking at old messages from agent Testado, missed calls, etc... L He thought about calling him and getting him to testify on Antonio in his son's murder. Help authenticate his voice from the call made to him the night of his son's murder.

He wanted to get back bad. He may have to settle with getting even with Garcia because he was the one who put the hit on him and his son. No doubt about it and he'll run into him. He's thinking better yet he'll find him no matter what it takes and face off with him.

Chapter 42

DALLAS, TEXAS

Garcia and his son had been riding around being chauffeured in a royal blue Rolls Royce Phantom Ghost discussing business. Garcia hadn't done anything since he'd been out. Renaldo had been laying low since the feds captured Antonio. He was one of their main players so they had a feeling that the Feds were breathing down Renaldo's neck.

Sure enough, Garcia was being watched.

"So, when do you think is a good time to crank back up." Asked Renaldo.

"After Antonio's trial which is soon. I'm trying to free him?

"Free him, how are you gonna do that pops?

"I'm going to come up with something." Said Garcia. "you don't run into people like Antonio all the time. Got to keep him or get him free!" Said Garcia.

"How are the lawyers talking? Asked Renaldo.

Garcia grinned and twitched in the seat to that question.

"It doesn't look too good." Said Garcia.

"There's no way to get to the witnesses? Asked Renaldo.

"After all that has happened, I doubt it.

"So, what are you thinking about? Breaking him out?"
"Yeah!" Answered Garcia.

Chicago

7:00 P.M.

D'Ant had contacted his people like his father suggested.

Garcia got back to him shortly and told him. "After the trial."

Simple as that D'Anthony accepted the message in his mind as a sign to stay patient.

Meanwhile, he was at a Bull's basketball game with his girl. Chilling and enjoying the game when someone tapped his shoulder almost making him jump out of his seat. He quickly looked back to see who it was and to his surprise, it was his old mentor and old plug/ O.G. from his hood G-Rock!

"Wusup, D'Ant? Good to see you back we got a lot to talk about."

D'Ant answered. "Yeah, we do."

A week later

Atlanta, GA

Federal Courthouse

It was showtime! Time for my trial to kick off or should I say our trial. Motions had been submitted to have our trials separate. I thought the judge would do that because the trial would be longer and better for publicity. Ain't no telling how this would turn out and that's no lie. I was kind of nervous on the strength of all these rats. Motherfuckas not keeping it real and it was hard as hell to get to the witnesses or jurors.

After all the shit that happened and my reputation, the government wasn't taking any chances.

"Antonio Deangelo!" Hollered at one of the CO's as they were approaching my cell.

"No need to holla um up and ready!"

Two CO's approached my cell and put handcuffs, belly chains, and shackles on my feet like a slave. I hated like a fuck that I had got caught up again.

"Man, the media are like animals out there." Said one of the CO's.

"Bru, if you beat this case you'll put me on in the rap game? You said you would my nigga." Said the CO.

He had been looking out for me by bringing me cigarettes, weed, and cell phones. In turn, I had his pockets fat. One of the female CO's liked me and ole boy set it up for me to fuck her.

"Yea, I got you my nigga. Even if I lose I'll get you signed to my son's record label when he kicks back off. If not, I'll holler at one of these industry niggaz to put you on. My word is my bond."

"Bet, my nigga you good people. I can tell you ain't the monster they make you out to be. I wish you luck in the trial."

"Thanks!" I said. The whole time he was talking I was wondering about the big Chicano C.O. He was quiet and serious-looking as a fuck, but it was something about him like maybe I'd seen him before. Then he had this gangster swagger about him. I don't know. Anyway, they led me to the courtroom and when I entered cameras and lights were everywhere. I see what the CO was talking about. They led me past the prosecutor's table to the defense table where my legal team was. They stood up to greet me and they made sure the CO's took the cuffs and belly chains off me. They left the shackles on as I sat down and listened to my lawyers as they explained their strategy to me again.

"All rise!" Screamed the bailiff as the judge came out of his chambers and approached the bench.

"You may be seated!" Said federal Judge Barrett Thomas. "This is case #018-339-760. The United States vs defendant Antonio Deangelo et al with co-defendants. We'll get to them later. Is the government prepared?" Said the judge.

"Yes, your honor."

"Okay!"

"What about the defense? Are you all prepared to make your opening statements?"

"Yes, we are!"

"Well, let's have it!" Said the judge.

"Showtime!" I mumbled under my breath to my lawyers.

THE END

AUTOBIOGRAPHY

Author, Corey Bryant is 48 yrs old. Corey Bryant was born in Opelika, Alabama. As a child, Corey enjoyed reading all kinds of books and magazines. At the age of 19, Corey was incarcerated in the state of Alabama prison system. After serving about 3 yrs. he started writing but didn't get serious until he served 20 yrs in jail. That's when he wrote and completed yielding 2 unfulfilled Desires Vol. 1 and part of vol. 2 and R.I.C.O vol. 1 Corey still enjoys reading and writing and spending time with family and friends. Corey resides in Opelika, Alabama.